Praise for Charlene Teglia's
Miss Lonely Hearts

"I have yet to read a story by Charlene Teglia that I do not love, and this author has done it again. With her own special blend of humor and sex appeal, she has delivered a delightful little romance guaranteed to warm even the coldest of nights – whether you live in Alaska or not!"

~ *CK2S Kwips and Kritiques*

"Jason and Cassandra are great characters. ...The chemistry between the two is hot! The by-play between the two was electric and the internal dialog was fascinating and fun to read. I hope that Ms. Teglia brings us back to this small Alaskan town with more of their stories. This is a book I would definitely recommend to a friend looking for quick pick-me-up read."

~ *Fallen Angel Reviews*

"I really enjoyed this story. The author does not overload it with extra characters and makes each and every one of the quirky denizens of The Last Resort special, even the interchangeable and silent Lawrence twins...This is a warm and funny story that I will definitely read again and if we gave out half cups this would get 4 ½ cups for sure."

~ *Coffee Time Romance*

Look for these titles by
Charlene Teglia

Now Available:

The Gripping Beast
Night Music
Night Rhythm

Print Anthology:
Beginnings

Miss Lonely Hearts

Charlene Teglia

A Samhain Publishing, Ltd. publication.

Samhain Publishing, Ltd.
577 Mulberry Street, Suite 1520
Macon, GA 31201
www.samhainpublishing.com

Miss Lonely Hearts
Copyright © 2009 by Charlene Teglia
Print ISBN: 978-1-59998-833-7
Digital ISBN: 1-59998-031-2

Editing by Angela James
Cover by Scott Carpenter

First Samhain Publishing, Ltd. electronic publication: October 2007
First Samhain Publishing, Ltd. print publication: June 2009

Dedication

For all those who've taken a gamble on love and hit the jackpot. The world needs happily ever afters.

Chapter One

"This has nothing to do with you, Cassandra. It's not personal. It's business."

For a frozen moment, Cassandra Adams could only stare in stricken silence as the incomprehensible words reverberated in her head. Then the meaning sank in. It was business, all right, and she would bet her last dollar that Riley the Bastard was at the bottom of it. Which made it very personal.

Tom was dumping her. A month before their planned wedding day. Less than two months before her deadline. What were the odds that the perfect man would suddenly decide somebody else was the perfect woman without any warning? Riley had gotten to him, just like he'd gotten to her first fiancé. The bastard.

If she looked like Morticia Addams, this wouldn't be happening, Cass thought. She imagined trading her too-wholesome face, blonde hair and blue eyes for the dark and dangerous look. Slinky and seductive and elegant. More like a woman of the world, a force to be reckoned with. Less like a future soccer mom.

Tom would be too afraid of Morticia to pull a stunt like this, in public, while she was at work, no less. Of course, if she were Morticia, she'd have Gomez. Gomez would never ditch her while she was working, or less than two months before she had to be married or lose everything to Riley the Bastard.

The Adams family she'd been born into could be very good at scary, Cass had reason to know, but lacked the humor that made the fictional Addamses so endearing. Riley was ruthless and he probably thought he was going to win.

Damned if she'd let him. Although at the moment, she didn't have a plan to counter this move. She was going to need a plan. Soon. Time was running out.

Cass watched as the impeccably dressed man she'd been engaged to five minutes earlier adjusted first his tie, then his cuffs in studied motions. All designed to look as if he was relaxed but in reality no doubt calculated to keep from looking her in the eye. Maybe he *was* a little bit afraid of her. She could hope.

He didn't look the least bit heartbroken, though. Had she truly believed this animated suit loved her? Or had she just heard what she wanted to hear, seen what she wanted to see?

She'd wanted to believe his passionless manner was simply reserve, not lack of feeling. She'd wanted to see Tom as a solid, responsible individual because she wanted someone to depend on after Matthew.

The realization was chilling, but in retrospect it seemed obvious to Cassandra that she'd chosen someone the total opposite of the flashy, smooth-talking charmer who'd deserted her at the altar for the other woman Riley pushed in his path, along with a hefty bribe.

Only Tom wasn't so different, after all.

Tom, the man so conservative and aloof she would have sworn he'd be thrilled to have any woman committed to him to rescue him from loneliness, was dumping her to marry his boss's daughter.

Riley's daughter. Cass ground her teeth together. Why

hadn't she anticipated this? She should have known Tom was too easy to get to, working for Adams Imports. She should have realized Riley would use the same tactics that had worked so well to break up her first engagement to sabotage the second. But even after she'd realized that Riley was utterly ruthless and had no intention of playing fair, she'd still believed Tom loved her and wouldn't be lured away as easily as Matthew had been.

Clearly she'd been wrong.

Maybe she'd made a mistake, not telling Tom what was at stake if they married. He didn't know the whole story. From the outside, she looked like the poor relative in the Adams family, not an heiress. Then again, did she want a husband she could buy? And did she want to keep her inheritance from falling into Riley's control only to risk losing half in divorce court? If Tom was willing to marry just to better himself, what would stop him from marrying her long enough to be entitled to half her assets?

Good thing he was marrying Carol instead. And he'd have to keep working for Riley. Those two things were almost punishment enough to make Cass feel better about being dumped a few weeks before her wedding. Almost.

As if watching the scene unfold from a remote vantage point, disconnected from the people involved, Cass heard Tom go on to say, "You know I don't have any choice. Carol is the perfect corporate wife. But it doesn't have to change our relationship unless you let it."

Cass gave a short, unamused laugh. "I'm pretty sure bigamy is against the law, Tom."

Tom compressed his lips in a firm line. "You're making this very difficult."

"Imagine that," she drawled. "I'm making it hard for you to tell me you're marrying someone else but you'd still like to— what, exactly? Would I officially be a kept woman, or would it be more of a spontaneous, no-strings occasional sex arrangement?"

Somewhere in the back of her mind, she was privately amazed she could sound so calm when her heart was being publicly hacked right down the center without anesthesia and her future potentially destroyed. Although, as she said the words, she realized she wasn't going to miss the sex, which was already occasional and not very spontaneous. That was telling.

Tom finally looked her in the eye and the coldness there wasn't even the cold of anger. It was simply dismissal. She didn't exist for him, on an emotional level or any level. How long had that been true? And why hadn't she noticed sooner? The sex alone should have been a clue.

"Maybe it's best if we simply say good-bye," he stated. "You're overreacting."

Overreacting? Cass's lips twisted in wry amusement. She wondered what Tom would have said if he'd witnessed her breaking the floral arrangement for the altar over Matthew's head the morning of her last wedding that wasn't.

Her only regret, in retrospect, was that it had been a real waste of the flowers.

"Yes, I think we should say good-bye," Cass answered. They should never have said hello. And he shouldn't have done this to her at the restaurant she worked at, where he obviously had hoped to avoid a scene. "I do have a going away present for you, though."

She lifted the pitcher of water she'd just brought to his table and upended it in an endless, glorious, frigid stream over his designer suit. She hoped it was the most expensive one he owned. Since money and symbols of success seemed to be the only things dear to Tom's heart, she wanted the satisfaction of hitting him where it would hurt.

The icy baptism struck her as an appropriate final farewell to the cold man. Only a man colder than an iceberg could do what he'd just done. It was only fitting that he got an ice treatment from her in return.

"Ahem."

Cass closed her eyes in horror and knew without even looking the manager of the trendy Seattle restaurant was right behind her. The one who'd had it in for her since she'd started the job. And she'd just handed him the excuse he'd been waiting for to get rid of her.

She turned slowly. With a kind of nightmare quality that rendered the entire scene somehow unreal, she heard the manager saying in quiet, even tones, "You're fired."

Somehow, she found herself outside and walking in something of a daze. She'd lost her fiancé. She'd lost her job. If she didn't do something about it, she stood to lose her entire future.

And it had all happened so fast.

Cass came to a sudden halt as she considered something else—she didn't have much in the way of savings. Riley's combined harassment and influence had made countless jobs end, doors close and unexpected expenses mount. Which was why she'd ended up working as a waitress despite her college degree, earning half what she was capable of making.

Cass mentally took stock. No job, no fiancé, practically no savings. She also didn't have a very reliable alternative source of income, since her freelance photography was a long ways from being able to pay the bills in spite of a steady stream of sales and credits. And she could bet that her name would now be mud at all the high-end restaurants.

She could always go work at a diner or truck stop, but the money wouldn't come close to what she'd made at The Atrium.

And that was barely enough to survive Seattle's high cost of living. Not to mention the high cost of dog food at the rate Rex went through it.

What a mess. And it was all she'd seemed to make of her life so far. Where had she gone wrong?

By moving to Seattle, Cassandra, she told herself as it started to rain. It comforted her, in an odd kind of way. She could count on the miserable rain in Seattle. Since she couldn't seem to count on anything else, she'd take comfort where she could.

One thing she'd counted on, moving from her small hometown on Washington's Olympic Peninsula to the big city, was the opportunity to meet more people and have more potential mates to choose from along with more potential photography clients and contacts. But so far, more relationship choices only seemed to mean more potential for dating disaster. And being closer to Riley meant it was easier for him to sabotage her progress if it looked like she was getting too close to the altar.

She'd been so close, both times.

Maybe she should have stayed home. But Port Townsend, Washington, didn't provide much in the way of choices, disastrous or otherwise. By the time she was sixteen, she'd known there wasn't a single person in all of Jefferson County she could see herself settling down with.

Settling down. Babies, Cassandra thought wistfully. A home and family. She wanted kids and couldn't remember a time when she hadn't. When she'd been younger, she'd taken it for granted it would just happen and it would be easy. She would never have guessed it would be this hard to fall in love and get married. Already she'd been through two failed engagements and a string of dead-end relationships and she was about to turn twenty-eight, which meant she was almost out of time.

She really didn't think she could face going through another failed relationship even if the clock wasn't ticking. In fact, the possibility that she could have another ten years of dating roulette ahead of her made her want to throw up. Not to mention the hard fact that fertility rates went down and pregnancy risks went up with every year that went by. If it took another ten years to find the right man, it could be too late. She could end up missing out on the children she wanted by default.

It seemed she hadn't given the marriage and family goal enough attention. She'd left it up to nature while she obsessed over F stops, photo effects and the pursuit of getting paid for her art form. She'd thought she had plenty of time. She wasn't at all opposed to marriage. She'd thought it would be easy to meet her birthday deadline.

Of course, in the early days she hadn't expected that Riley wouldn't play fair, either. She'd assumed she could become a world-class photographer, fall in love, get married and secure her inheritance without opposition. Looking back over the last ten years it was almost painful to believe she'd once been so naïve.

Cass summoned her pride and forced her legs to get moving. Okay, so, romance hadn't worked out yet. She wasn't unworthy of love. Somewhere out there was a man she could love who would love her and who'd love to have a family. Her problem was that she was going about it all wrong.

The thought jelled as she reached her apartment and let herself in. There wasn't anything wrong with her, she'd just picked the wrong men. Men who didn't really share her goals.

And maybe she'd been unrealistic, focusing on the romantic relationship instead of practicalities. She didn't have time for romance now. She had less than two months to get married. She didn't need a man who would say, "I love you" nearly as much as she needed one who could be counted on to say "I do" and not back out.

Maybe what she needed to do was to approach this the way she probably should have from the beginning, more like a career move. If she'd put half the effort into finding the right man that she'd put into learning her way around film and a camera, she might have more to show for her personal life. If learning an art form and building a career out of it didn't just happen, why had she thought the right relationship would?

Maybe it was easier to find a good career than a good man, but still, the same principle applied, didn't it? She could approach relationships in a totally different way. Take a more practical approach.

One thing was clear. It was time to put aside the impractical daydream that true love would just fall out of the clear blue sky and land at her feet. Unless she wanted to let Riley win, it was time to start a systematic search for a marriage-minded family man.

Men like Matthew were quick to make promises, but that was all they were good for—empty promises. On the other hand, men like Tom were too dedicated to climbing the corporate ladder to ever put their families first. So now that she'd visited both extremes, maybe she could find some sort of middle ground.

There had to be something more lasting than attraction. Something more substantial. And there had to be something more meaningful to base a relationship on.

Something like commitment. There was something neither of her exes could claim to possess. Friendship. Common goals and values. Those were the things she should look for, because they'd last long after the honeymoon was over.

What was love, anyway? Did anyone really know? Did any two people mean the same thing when they said those words?

She'd already heard enough declarations of love to last a lifetime, and she was living in an apartment with her dog instead of living in a home with a family of her own. If what she'd seen so far was love, then it obviously didn't go hand in hand with marriage and it definitely didn't last.

In a way, she supposed she owed Riley for breaking up those relationships before they got to the altar. Any man who could be bought or brought to heel by Riley Adams' money and influence wasn't the kind of man she wanted to marry, let alone bring a child into the world with.

Maybe the old idea of love coming after marriage wasn't far off. After choosing the right person, the mechanics of building a life together had to lead to something. Enduring affection, if nothing else. Companionship. Shared experiences.

Maybe she'd just gone about this backwards. Maybe she should look for a husband and expect it to lead to love, instead of falling in love and expecting it to lead to a husband.

At the very least, she'd be taking a step towards the life she wanted for herself instead of hanging on by a thread in this dreary city. Well, maybe that was unfair. The Sound was beautiful and even the fog could be appealing in its own way. The nearby Olympic Peninsula and the Hoh Rain Forest had a unique, lush beauty she'd enjoyed countless times on meandering walks and photo safaris.

She just had unhappy memories associated with this place, and that was her own fault. The moss-covered soil of Seattle wasn't to blame for her bad choices.

Still, Cass couldn't help the deep conviction it was time to move on and shake the dust off.

Or shake the rain off, anyway, she thought with a faint trace of returning humor. A good sign. It meant her heart wasn't crushed. A little battered and dented, maybe, but she had too much pride to cry over the kind of man who'd dump her without hesitation to advance his career.

She really ought to look at this as a blessing in disguise. She should be glad she'd found out what Tom was really like in time to prevent an irrevocable mistake. Just like she should be glad she'd found out about Matthew after the rehearsal, not after the wedding. She was hurt, but at least there weren't any innocent children suffering along with her.

She also told herself the dampness streaking her face came from the endless drizzle outdoors, not from her eyes.

She was practical now and a practical woman didn't cry over lost loves that weren't and romantic daydreams that wouldn't be and the sharks that were all the family she had left.

A practical woman would dry her eyes so she could see straight and then go get busy looking for middle ground.

Exactly what she was going to do.

Just as soon as it stopped raining.

Jason Alexander looked up from the dull and repetitive task of polishing the shiny oak bar top when the door of The Last Resort swung open. Good, a customer. Something to do, something to relieve the tedium, someone to talk to.

Until he realized the two large men making their ponderous way to the padded barstools were Dwight and Duke Lawrence.

The twins never talked. It was an amazing phenomenon, but true, nevertheless. Jason had wondered at it from the first time he'd seen them take those same seats on his first night in residence as the new owner of The Last Resort.

They hadn't shown the least bit of surprise that the place had changed hands, or any interest in his identity. They'd simply waited until one of the other locals piped up and told him they always had one shot of bourbon and one draft apiece.

Never one to back down from a challenge, Jason had summoned his considerable charm and slid the beverages in front of them with a smile and a friendly greeting.

Silence. The only sound came when Duke rustled a bill in paying the tab. Even the raising and lowering of the glasses occurred in an incredible silence, the heavy restaurant glass never clunking when it made contact with the oak bar, but settling gently on the cocktail napkins without a whisper. That this feat of steady, soundless movement came from two men big enough to be mistaken for a pair of Yeti was nothing short of miraculous.

The tandem performance had amazed Jason then, and it amazed him now. Sometimes he wondered if they even realized the bar had changed hands. The previous owner, Lucky Day, had been abandoned by his namesake in Reno. The outcome of that fateful poker game had left Jason Alexander, professional gambler extraordinaire, the sole proprietor of a rustic bar in Southeast Alaska.

Maybe, he thought with a flash of wicked humor, they couldn't tell the difference because all bartenders looked alike in the dark.

Not that it was all that dark just then. It was only spring, but already the days were visibly lengthening. The bar's traditional dim lighting was highly augmented by the sun, streaming in through the small windows at full strength. That was one of the things he truly loved about the area. In the summer, the extended daylight lent everyone a kind of exuberance that made up for the long, dark winters. Nobody slept or stayed inside if they could help it.

In fact, the restless energy of this little city on the Tongass Narrows with the dubious honor of being named Alaska's Rain Capital had appealed to his adventure-loving soul immediately.

From the moment he'd stepped off the ferry, he'd felt like he'd come home.

Here, in a place with a history of gold rushes, on a little plot of land in the former red-light district, was a place a gambler and wanderer could settle down in as easily as he could settle behind a blackjack table.

It fit him and he'd made up his mind immediately, with a gambler's sure instincts, that he wasn't selling The Last Resort. Or putting it up as collateral, either. He was leaving the life of plush hotels and room service behind forever. He was twenty-eight years old and it was time he had a home.

So Jason had taken up his position behind the bar and never looked back. Two years later, he wasn't sorry.

But he still hadn't ever managed to get a word out of Dwight or Duke in all that time. He only knew which was which because Duke always sat on the left. Also, his well-developed powers of personal observation had detected very slight differences that distinguished one from the other. Dwight sported a faint scar on one cheek and Duke had thicker brows. Still, they were as identical as it was probably possible to get without actually being one and the same person.

But something about them was different tonight. Jason studied the two dour faces as he served the usual drinks with a flourish. "On the house this time, Duke," he said, knowing it was the left-hand twin's turn to buy. They traded off, another well-established ritual they never deviated from.

He thought he actually saw a glimmer of surprise in the man's pale eyes. "You're welcome," he responded, as if Duke

20

had spoken instead of nearly blinking.

With these two, body language was about as verbal as he could expect

"Least I can do for you two, since you're looking so down," Jason went on. Dwight definitely twitched as he reached for the bourbon. Interesting. Now what could these two be bothered about? Jason pondered the possibilities. Probabilities were his forte.

Odds were, they'd finally gotten tired of each other's companionship and gotten lonely in a purely masculine way. That being the case, and being as alike as they were, the two had probably then settled their affections on the same woman.

"Woman trouble does that to us all," Jason stated in commiseration. "We men have to stick together. Though in your case, I don't recommend you take that too literally. The law doesn't recognize three-way marriages." Although employers and official agencies were recognizing every other kind of arrangement these days, and polyamorous groups weren't exactly unheard of. Live and let love. But the law was conservative.

Both Dwight and Duke rattled their shot glasses when they replaced them on the heavy oak slab. Jackpot!

"You know, you two might try asking her to choose between you." He offered the suggestion in the time-honored spirit of supportive advice from the bartender to his burdened patrons. Dwight and Duke were apparently unacquainted with the custom personally, but he suspected they stopped in night after night mostly to listen to the talk, even if they didn't participate actively.

Now, as lacking in verbal skills as they were, how likely was it they'd ever actually say something like that to a woman? It was amazing that they'd even gotten as far as saying hello. Too amazing, Jason realized. Which meant that they hadn't. Which meant they'd been doing their wooing in silence. Which meant...

"Of course, maybe you shouldn't do a thing like that through the mail. It might go better in person."

Then it happened.

Dwight's big fist curled up and thumped the bar in a single, silent shout of frustration and despair. And he spoke.

"Too late. She dumped us both."

The rusty admission drew a nod of agreement and pure misery from Duke who chimed in, "Jilted," in the heaviest, creakiest, rustiest voice Jason had ever heard.

Jilted. Now, that was serious. Jason eyed the two, surprised they'd proposed on paper. Well, not really. How else would they do it, unless they met a deaf woman and communicated by holding up a ring?

"You mean she agreed to marry both of you?" he asked as the implications of Duke's single contribution to the conversation sank in.

Two woeful heads nodded once. Two ham hands raised and lowered heavy beer mugs in unison.

Jason would have given an awful lot to meet the woman who'd do that, he really would. Imagine. Taking on the two Lawrence men. The two enormous Lawrence men. The mind boggled. Whoever she was, she was truly an adventurous soul. Although it seemed she'd thought better of her decision to walk on the wild side at the last minute.

"Well, at least you found out about her in time," Jason offered.

Two heads hung low.

Now what did that mean? He swiftly concluded it meant they'd lost more than their hearts. Jason's former life began to pass before his eyes, and the words *con artist* rang in his head. "My friends," he said, "you have just been done in by Miss Lonely Hearts."

Two heads rose. Four brows shot upward.

An explanation was requested, evidently.

"Miss Lonely Hearts is an old con. One of the safest, actually. It's small potatoes, hard to trace and usually unreported." He saw he had their full attention, and continued. "Here's how it works. She sees a lonely hearts ad, and picks a victim. She writes love letters to set the coldest heart on fire and sends a picture of the most heartbreakingly beautiful woman you've ever seen. She also confesses to being on hard times and asks for the airfare to join her groom."

Two mouths set in a hard line and two paws curled around the mugs with enough controlled force to break the glass. The equivalent in more verbal men of shouting raging accusations and hurling abuse. All things considered, though, he thought they were taking it pretty well.

"Then she takes the money and runs. Literally. Don't blame yourselves, men, she's smart and almost impossible to catch because she never gets greedy. A little here, a little there, never in the same place."

Another voice joined in the conversation. "Not exactly, Jason. Pour me a double, will you?"

Jason looked up in surprise to see Sam Weiss, the high school English teacher looking as hurt and as sheepish as the Lawrence brothers.

"Not you, too, Sam?"

The man nodded. "You know how it is here, Jason. Ketchikan isn't all that big, and we're on an island. We get the cruise ships and the tourists coming through from May to September, but winter's a different story. Not many visitors

23

want to stay on, and plenty of people move here and then change their minds after the first winter. It's not surprising some of us start to look for a bride online."

Now that was a little too coincidental to ring true to Jason. The odds were very much against three of his regulars being hit by a con artist at random. He began to wonder just who Miss Lonely Hearts was really after.

"Same deal? Same picture?"

Sam turned to Dwight and Duke. "Beautiful blonde. Eyes the color of lapis lazuli. She wrote poetry so beautiful I cried."

Two mugs hit the oak slab with angry force.

Sam turned back to Jason. "Yes, same woman, all right. From Seattle. I sent her a ticket and she never came, but the airline confirmed the ticket had been cashed in."

Seattle. He didn't remember anyone who had a grudge against him in that area. In fact, Jason didn't remember anyone who had a grudge against him, period. Even Lucky Day, the bar's not-so-lucky former owner, had been glad to get free of The Last Resort. He'd claimed he was tired of staying in one place. He'd traveled around the lower forty-eight awhile, then headed for the Yukon, the last time Jason had heard.

"She broke my heart," Sam went on. "I thought there must have been an accident, or a family emergency. I tried to write to her again, but the emails bounced and the letter I sent to the postal address got returned."

Dwight jerked his head in Sam's direction, indicating he wanted to buy Sam's drink.

Amazing. Miss Lonely Hearts had brought the Lawrence brothers out of their cone of silence and had them interacting.

She had Sam nearly crying in his whisky, and he was a known cynic with a preference for the bleakest literature in the history of the written word, a man who scoffed at romance.

She'd hit The Last Resort, and hit it hard.

Determination fired in Jason's heart.

She wasn't going to get away with it.

She'd thrown down the gauntlet, but he was going to pick it up and stuff it down her beautiful throat. Although it was highly unlikely Miss Lonely Hearts was actually the woman in the picture.

Whoever she was, the mystery woman wasn't going to set up an operation on his turf and fleece his friends.

"Watch the bar for me, will you, Sam?" Jason asked, tossing his bar towel on the shiny oak surface. "I believe I have a personal ad to go and place."

He started towards the stairs that led to his living space above the bar and his computer, then turned back to ask, "Which website?"

Sam answered and the Lawrence brothers nodded agreement.

"Got it." Jason went on his way, determined to set a trap and provide the juiciest bait.

Namely, the kind of ad a con couldn't resist.

An invitation to Miss Lonely Hearts to come and get his wallet.

He'd write a lonely plea for a mail-order mate that would melt a heart of stone and trap the foolish grifter who'd made the fatal mistake of getting greedy. He'd send a ticket when she asked, all right, but he'd be there to bring her in when she tried to cash it.

She wasn't really all that clever.

She shouldn't have challenged a gambler to a game of hearts.

Chapter Two

"Cass? Open up, it's Lisa."

The voice was accompanied by staccato pounding on the door and a welcoming woof from Rex. Cass ran a hand through her disheveled hair and went to let her friend in.

"Hi," she said. She stood clear to let Lisa pass. Rex crowded into the doorway to snuffle at the visitor, probably hoping to sniff out dog biscuits. When he didn't find any, he went back to collapse in disappointment by his food dish. That or he just felt he'd done his canine duty and nothing more was required of him.

"Hi." Lisa's sharp hazel eyes took in the puffy evidence of tears and she quickly offered a hug. "Oh, Cass, I heard what happened. That Tom, what a jerk. And getting you fired, too."

Cass felt a flash of pride stiffen her spine and she groped for some shred of dignity. "I didn't get fired, I quit." Then she slumped down again. "I don't think Tom meant to get me fired, he just didn't think I'd make a scene. Anyway, it's over."

Lisa snorted. "He came to tell you he'd decided you weren't good enough for him so he was marrying somebody else, and he didn't think you'd make a scene?"

Cass felt her lips twitch. Put that way, it was ridiculous. And proof positive he'd never really known her. "Carol probably never makes scenes."

"Carol probably doesn't have a pulse. Cass, I'm sorry." Lisa patted her shoulder in a comforting gesture. "But don't worry, you'll find a better man. Better than Tom. I never liked him anyway. You'll fall madly in love. Then you'll live happily ever after with six kids and a station wagon in the suburbs, and your husband will love every picture you take."

Cass had to smile at the description of her wildest fantasy come true. Some fantasy. Maybe if she wasn't so wholesome, so, well, *boring*, she wouldn't be here. Dumped. Again. Although maybe her fantasy of becoming a famous photographer balanced out the domestic bliss fantasy.

She thought of the sex life she wouldn't be missing with Tom and frowned. Then again, maybe she needed better fantasy material in her personal life. While she was fixing her life, she might as well fix everything.

She decided to keep that thought to herself, though. "No, Lisa, I've given up on falling madly in love," she informed her friend and former coworker at The Atrium.

The only good thing that had come from the job, aside from the money, had been meeting Lisa Atkins, a struggling musician making ends meet by waiting tables during lunch.

In Lisa, she'd found a kindred spirit. A fellow dreamer, unwilling to settle for less than what she wanted out of life and willing to do whatever it took to make it happen. Lisa worked long and hard, performing and then breaking down and moving equipment until three or four in the morning if it was a local gig, later if it was at a distance, then getting up in time to be at work at eleven the next morning. Cass admired her tenacity. She'd make it in the highly competitive industry because she simply refused to quit, and when the going got tough, she worked harder.

Like Cass herself. She wasn't quitting, not by a long shot.

All the disappointments she'd encountered so far just hardened her resolve and fed her determination. She refused to accept that the life she wanted wasn't going to happen. If she wanted something, she had to create an opportunity and then make it work. She'd wanted to be a photographer, and little by little she was making it happen. She wanted a family, a real one, and she could make that happen, too. People did, all over the world. It wasn't an impossible dream.

Most of all, she wasn't going to fail to meet her birthday deadline and give the other Adams the satisfaction of seeing her beaten.

Lisa was looking disturbed so Cass gave her what she hoped was a reassuring smile as she went on to explain, "I have a better idea. I've decided I've been doing this backwards. Instead of looking for love and hoping it'll lead to marriage, I'm going to look for a husband I can love."

"What exactly are you saying?" Lisa demanded, tucking strands of straight brown hair behind her ears.

"I'm saying, this time the cart goes behind the horse."

Lisa threw up her hands in exasperation. "You and your quaint farm sayings."

Cass wrinkled her nose. "Rural, not farm. I've never lived on a farm."

"Same difference, to a city girl. Now explain yourself." Lisa folded her arms and waited.

"I've decided the only way to get what I want from a relationship is to find the man who wants the same things," Cass explained. "A man who wants to get married and have a family. A stable man, supportive of my career choice, who's ready and willing to commit."

Lisa gave her a guarded look. "I see. Well, actually, I don't. But go on."

28

"It's fairly simple, Lisa. I'm going to be a mail-order bride."

Silence.

"You're really serious, aren't you? Cass, you have to know how risky this is. You're talking about marrying a total stranger. He could be anything, a murderer, an escaped convict. Do you realize what kind of a chance you're taking?" Lisa's hazel eyes were wide with distress and her arms waved in ever wider and sharper motions as her emotions escalated.

"Yes, I'm serious, and yes, I've thought this through," Cass answered patiently. "It's not like I'm jumping out of an airplane without a parachute. You should know me better than that."

"That's not a rural saying," Lisa grumbled. "Don't mix your metaphors on me."

Cass grinned. "Just checking, you might not have been listening. I'm not talking about blindly hopping on a plane to marry some stranger. I'm going to correspond, exchange pictures, then meet him in person. If he's horrible, I'll break it off and come back. Or stay on there, whatever. I've really had it with this place, to tell you the truth."

And she had. Seattle, city of disillusionment. Well, for her, at least. To everyone else who lived there, it must have some profound attraction. Or maybe they just liked rain. Growing up in the rain shadow where she'd been protected from the region's downpour hadn't prepared her for Seattle's weather at all.

"You really want to leave?" Lisa's face turned tragic. "Oh, no. You'll start having kids and forget about me. Or decide it's anti-family to consort with a rock musician."

Cass laughed, glad Lisa had come to cheer her up. Amazing, she was actually laughing again. Proof that she was still alive and capable of recovering. Or maybe just proof her heart had known, deep down, that Tom wasn't the one for her and it had never fully been his. Aside from the anger and sense

29

of betrayal, there was a kind of peace now that it was over. As if a mistake had been corrected, however painfully, and now her life was back on track.

"No, that won't happen," she said to Lisa. "You'll come and visit whenever you're touring nearby, and the kids will think you're cool. They'll think I'm cool by association. I'll be the Cool Mom."

"Good plan, I like it. Not the other plan, though. I'm not crazy about this mail-order business," Lisa sighed.

"Come on, let's sit and be comfortable," Cass suggested, ushering her to the sitting area of the spacious studio apartment. One thing she did like about Seattle was this apartment. The open concept made it feel roomy and inviting in spite of the limited square feet. High ceilings and exposed beams were a legacy of the building's former industrial days. Large windows captured whatever sunlight the clouds were willing to let slip through.

She looked around, remembering her fever to decorate and the search for portable screens to section off portions of the room. She'd used large, pillowy chairs, tall plants and wicker tables to create the feeling of a tropical environment that cheered her up in the cold, dark winters. Cass felt a pang of nostalgia, surveying it. This was her first independent home, not counting an early shared apartment. The first place she'd made her own.

She was going to miss it, but she'd probably like her new home better. The one with the station wagon, the husband and the kids where she had it all, career and family. The one she needed to make for herself.

She curled in a comfortable rattan chair and tried to find the logical place to start. Lisa was the only person she'd taken into her confidence about the fact that her grandfather had left her money held in trust, but she'd never mentioned the amount. He'd cautioned her often enough to keep quiet about it when he was alive, and when she heard the terms he'd specified after his death, she actually understood his reasoning. She didn't agree with it, but she understood why it had seemed best to him.

If it was known that she stood to inherit a fortune, she'd be a target for unscrupulous men. If she'd already inherited before marrying, she'd be an even bigger target. She knew he'd honestly done it intending to protect her. Even if it did put her in a difficult position.

On the bright side, she wouldn't have to question the motives of any man who married her. She'd never have to worry if her only attraction was in the bank.

Cass took a breath and said, "There's something I have to tell you. I don't have all the time in the world to find a husband. I have until my twenty-eighth birthday."

Lisa perched opposite her. "Isn't that a little inflexible? Maybe your biological clock is ticking, but you'll still have eggs in another year."

"It's not my biological clock," Cass said. Then she imagined holding a baby a year from now and amended, "Well, maybe that, too. But the deadline isn't so much physical as legal. If I'm not married when I turn twenty-eight, I don't inherit. The money held in trust for me goes to Riley and family. They don't need it, and I do, and I want to get married anyway, so I intend to fulfill the terms."

Lisa opened and closed her mouth a couple of times. Finally, she said, "You have to get married to inherit? What kind of patriarchal rule is that?"

"Funny you should ask," Cass sighed. "My grandfather's will. The wisdom of the previous generation at work."

Lisa shook her head. "The plot thickens."

Cass thought about Riley's machinations and said, "You have no idea. Anyway, my birthday is coming up fast and my wedding just got cancelled. I don't have a lot of time to waste. I can either sit here crying about how unfair it is and let it all go to Riley, or I can go find a man, get married and get everything I want."

"Get even, too," Lisa said, visibly cheered. "I'm warming to this plan. Tell me more."

"First of all, I need to find a good couple-matching site. I'm going to search the personal profiles very carefully and separate out the men that look like possibilities. Then I'll send emails to the ones I think might lead somewhere. I'll narrow it down based on the responses I get, and go from there."

Lisa lifted one brow in distrust. "Sure. Then you'll be off to Bluebeard's castle, right?"

"Wrong, I'll know at least as much about him as I did about Tom. And Matthew."

Oh, it hurt to admit that. That she'd been so wrong, so blind, so unobservant. But she didn't think saying so would put Lisa's mind at ease, so she didn't mention it. Instead, she added, "Besides, this is partly my fault. I wasn't paying attention. I was busy earning a living and working on building a name as a photographer and I didn't see the signs that should have told me there were problems until it was over."

Signs like the fact that she couldn't remember the last time she and Tom had slept together. A month ago? More? That alone should have sounded a warning in her head.

"You have a point there," the lithe percussionist admitted. "It's not easy to balance career and relationships. This is why I have a battery-operated boyfriend." Lisa tapped out a beat on the chair arm as she considered Cass's plan. "This plan sounds workable. Just be careful. Have these guys investigated or something."

"Sure," Cass rolled her eyes. "Now that I'm unemployed, I'll just run right out and hire a private detective."

Lisa flushed. "Sorry. You are in a tight spot, aren't you?"

"No, I'll be okay. I have enough saved to get me through the next month at least, and I can always take a diner job." Cass vowed that her confidence wouldn't be misplaced, either. She could take care of herself. She'd be just fine. But getting into her chosen line of work had acquired a certain urgency. Maybe she could pick up a few extra freelance assignments in a hurry.

She'd been living too close to the edge as it was, barely making it and not contributing as much to her savings as she would have liked. Things might get a bit difficult, but her situation was far from hopeless. So she'd had some bad luck, helped along by antagonistic and greedy relatives. That didn't mean all was lost. Better days had to be ahead. She just had to hang in there and keep going.

She didn't intend to give up. She'd have a husband to keep her warm and children to love. A home to provide a safe haven from the storms of life. She'd have it, and she'd be happy, too.

Happiness was the best revenge.

And three million dollars in the bank never hurt anybody, either. She imagined never having to scrimp on film and processing again and came close to rubbing her hands together in anticipation. Photography was a very expensive art to practice, and the competition in the industry was fierce. Healthy financial backing could make the difference between success and failure in her chosen field.

"I know that look. That look means you've made up your mind and nothing will stop you," Lisa said. "Okay, since you're serious about this, I'll help. Also, I hate Riley and I hate the idea of him getting your money after sabotaging your engagement. Because I'm guessing that Tom turning up engaged to Carol instead of you just ahead of your deadline is not coincidence. We'll sign you up on the number one single's site on the web. Then we'll go through the candidates to find you the husband of your dreams."

The offer to help was a show of support that had Cass's eyes tearing up again. "Thanks, Lisa. You're the best friend anyone ever had."

"Yeah, I rock." The pert woman preened in a show of superiority that made them both burst out laughing.

Then Lisa sobered. "Funny, but now that your photography career is starting to take off and you're out to find your dream husband, I've got a line on something."

"I wouldn't say taking off, exactly, although I'm getting steady work now and I'm not going broke on film and processing anymore. But tell me about your news. Do you have a demo? An audition?"

"An audition. I think. A chance at one, anyway." Lisa took a deep breath and blew it out. "I heard Lorelei and the Sirens are replacing their drummer."

Cass let out a low whistle of appreciation. That wasn't just a shot at a dream, it *was* a dream. It didn't come any better than that. Rumor had it that Lorelei had the Midas touch of music—all her songs went gold. The Seattle-based group had burst onto the music scene from nowhere and taken it by storm.

"You're getting an audition with the Sirens? Lisa, that's incredible."

Lisa nodded, her usually animated face solemn. "It isn't a guarantee, but I'm in the running. And I just know I could do it. I want to do it. It's an incredible chance, not just because of the money but because of the difficulty. It's a real challenge."

Cass beamed at her friend. "That's the best news I've heard all day. Let's go get a latte and toast our dreams coming true."

"You're on!" Lisa stood and Cass led the way to the door. "We'll go to an internet café and start searching your singles ads, too. Might as well get started."

"No time like the present," Cass said. She who hesitated stood to lose an awful lot. Cass didn't intend to hesitate. "Does this mean I have to learn what all those abbreviations stand for?"

"Only if you don't want to end up writing to a woman," Lisa answered deadpan.

The two women exchanged looks and burst into laughter.

"I guess I'd better learn what the letters stand for," Cass decided demurely. "Is there an abbreviation for 'unable to commit'?"

"Hey, you're looking for a guy looking for a mail-order bride," Lisa reminded her. "How much more ready to commit can you get? Now, come on, grab your camera. You got dumped today, you might want to shoot something. Or somebody."

Now that Lisa mentioned it, she did feel like shooting somebody. Channeling that impulse into something constructive struck her as a good idea. Cass hung her Nikon around her neck. Then she filled the Kong toy with peanut butter and gave it to her dog as a consolation prize for leaving him home before heading out the door.

They walked the short distance to a neighborhood coffee shop and internet cafe and settled in with a couple of double lattes. Cass went through the site registration process and began to browse through search results for men around her age range who were specifically seeking marriage.

"Okay, what are your preferences?" Lisa asked as she watched Cass page down through the listings. "Any states you'd rule out, or would really like to live in?"

Cass thought it over. "I like being near the ocean. I've never lived very far away from it, so I guess I'd eliminate land-locked states. And away from here. I need a candidate Riley can't get to in time to stop the wedding."

"Okay, forget Interested in Iowa and Single in Seattle," Lisa replied. "Any other no-nos? There's really a lot to cover here, so you should narrow it down as much as you can."

"No men who just got divorced for the third time," Cass decided. "No inmates. No rabid religious extremist who'd forbid me to wear makeup, or want me to cover my hair." She thought about Rex, back at the apartment chewing on the Kong. "No animal haters."

"Sounds wise. Hey, what about Alaska?"

"What about Alaska?" Cass asked.

"I mean, would you be interested in moving there? There are lots of areas that aren't too heavily populated, and more that are pretty isolated. Lots of mail-order brides there. Would you mind living someplace remote?"

At the moment, the most remote corner of the world sounded pretty good, Cass thought. Someplace far from the endless drizzle and the relatives she'd prefer to never see again. But she had to admit it had merit as a suggestion even without those considerations. Alaska. Her breath nearly stopped as she considered it. The wildflowers. The mountains, the glaciers. Beauty, everywhere. Photographer's paradise.

"Sure, why not?" Cass said out loud.

Lisa tilted her head as she considered it. "The last frontier. Alaska would be an adventure, but are you sure about this? People move there and can't handle it."

36

"I'm used to rural, remember? I grew up in the town that rioted over Hollywood Video coming in. I can take the lack of urban amenities "

"True. Okay, Alaska's in. And look, there's a whole bunch of them. Lots of guys who spend summers on fishing boats, what about that?" Lisa asked, tapping her fingers against the table in an absent-minded drumming.

"No long-term absentee husbands," Cass said. "Some travel is fine, I'll probably have to do some myself. But not for months on end. I want a settled down kind of guy who wants to settle down with a wife."

Lisa nodded as Cass scrolled along, eliminating choices. "Well, we've narrowed it down, anyway. And you'll notice there's no abbreviation for Bluebeard, so read between the lines in those letters, okay?"

"Yes, Mom." Cass grinned, and realized her smile felt unforced. If she'd had any doubt this was the right thing to do, her gut reaction told her everything she needed to know. The further she went with this plan, the more positive she felt. Hopeful, not hesitant.

This was just like the time her dog got hit by a car, she reminded herself. She'd gone right out and gotten another one, after she cried and buried Daisy. It didn't mean she hadn't loved her Irish Setter. Just the opposite. She'd been afraid grief would paralyze her and prevent her from ever bonding with another dog.

In the same way, she couldn't stay stuck in the past now. The best thing, the healthy thing, was to look to the future and move on.

Her replacement mutt, Rex, had helped her get over Daisy's loss and made her smile again. By the same logic, a new love interest would help her get over the blow of being dumped and keep her from brooding over the untrustworthiness of men in general and her failure to pay attention to the signs of looming personal disaster in particular.

Well, she'd learned her lesson. She was paying attention now. And two bad apples didn't mean the rest should be judged accordingly. She wasn't going to give up on marriage because of Matthew and Tom.

She was going to find a decent, compatible man to marry, and that was final.

Cass took another sip of latte and wondered out loud, "So what are we down to?"

"Oh, only a few hundred possibilities," Lisa said, scanning the screen. "Here's one who needs someone to cook and clean for him. He doesn't come right out and say it, but close. 'ISO Betty Crocker' is close enough, wouldn't you say?"

Cass blinked. "ISO?"

"In Search Of. Old TV show. Seen the re-runs? No? Well, anyway, that's the abbreviation. So what do you say, Betty?"

Cass wrinkled her nose. "No, I don't think so. I actually don't mind domestic chores, but I'm interested in being a wife, not an indentured servant."

Lisa widened her eyes in pretended shock. "There's a difference?"

"Cynic. You just haven't seen the kinds of marriages I have. With the right husband, a marriage can be a very fulfilling partnership, so don't knock it."

"Okay, maybe I missed out on your rural upbringing and maybe I've dated one jerk too many. You say there are good ones out there, I'll give you the benefit of the doubt. For myself, I'll invest in long-life batteries. Hey, here's another one, and this is good. 'SWM seeks warm bride for cold northern nights'. What do you say?"

"Call General Electric," Cass muttered "Keep going."

"Hm 'Handsome Hunk ISO Lady Love. Chess players only'. Do you play chess?" Lisa arched a brow in inquiry, her hazel eyes sparkling with amusement.

Cass groaned. "Not one of those guys from the chess club. What kind of a man would require a chess-playing wife? No. Absolutely not."

"Picky, picky. No wonder you're still single. Oh, this is perfect." Suddenly serious, Lisa read, "'SWM ISO you, if you're ready for loving, committed marriage and willing to relocate to Alaska. Lonely independent business owner looking for lifemate. Attractive SWF, blonde preferred Come live with me and be my love.' "

Sure, and it was probably as real as the chess player who claimed to be a hunk. Still, the man didn't make any claims about his own appearance in the ad, he just requested an attractive mate. Well, why not? Men were visual, women wanted substance. Handsome wasn't the highest priority to her. After two disasters with handsome men, Cass was more than willing to consider a frog prince. Although he did have to be attractive at least to her.

They were going to exchange pictures, after all. If she couldn't imagine being able to respond to him physically, then she'd drop it. She'd had enough boring sex with Tom and she wasn't going to repeat the mistake of settling for a lifetime of that. But this man's ad struck a chord. It was worth writing an email to find out more.

"I take it the long silence means you're interested," Lisa remarked.

"I'm interested," Cass agreed. She looked past their table at the gray rain falling along the glass. Alaska was cold and snowy, but at least she'd be out of the rain. That was a plus.

"Well, then, here it is." Lisa reached over and hit Print. "You can email him from home and let me know what happens."

Cass eyed the printed out ad again in pensive silence. Did it represent the man of her dreams, or a dud? There was only one way to find out. She'd have to do a digital scan of the self-portrait she'd taken recently and fire up the email program on her computer.

And while she was at it, she'd Google to find out just where, exactly, Ketchikan, Alaska was.

When she found out an hour later, it didn't tell her much.

Apparently, it sat on a strip of land between the mountains and the sea on the Southeast Passage. On the western coast of an island she would never dare try to pronounce, Revillagigedo.

Cass considered the information she'd turned up on an internet search. He definitely lived in a rural area. It was accessible only by boat, ferry or plane, and it was the salmon capital of the world. If she fished, that would be a huge attraction.

She gave an inner philosophical shrug. The geographic isolation meant they'd be forced to work things out any time they argued. They'd be stuck together long enough for the hottest temper to cool in between outward-bound traffic runs.

Cass opened up an email window and wondered what to say. *Ruthless relatives are sabotaging my relationships and attempting to block my inheritance. Please propose and rescue me* had the benefit of honesty, but there was such a thing as too much honesty.

What did that leave for openers? Two-time jiltee would love

to marry you? Or any man, for that matter, as long as it's fast?

No, now she was being negative and ridiculous. She still had high standards, and she wouldn't compromise them to marry somebody who was totally wrong for her. The whole point was that she didn't want to marry just anybody. She was after the right somebody and she wanted to weed out the wrong ones before she got all emotional about them and let that confuse the issue. If he wasn't as wonderful as he sounded, she'd drop it. And even if he faked her out in email, she'd meet him in person to see if he was for real. It should be obvious pretty soon if he'd misrepresented himself.

She mulled it over, staring at the blank page, until Rex whined.

"What's the matter, puppy?" Cass asked, turning her head towards the hopelessly ugly mutt.

He picked up his leash and headed over to her chair, tail wagging hopefully, big eyes pleading.

"Okay, we'll go for a walk. I wasn't getting anywhere with this, anyway."

She suited action to words. With the leash snapped on to the collar and a plastic bag stuffed in her pocket to clean up after him, Cass picked up her keys and led him outside. One of the advantages of an apartment on ground level, she reflected. It didn't take long to get an anxious dog outdoors.

Walking Rex twice a day served to keep her in shape as a bonus. In a city, she didn't feel comfortable walking alone much. A dog as ugly as hers discouraged an awful lot of the street types who might have bothered her otherwise. His size probably helped, too.

Thinking of his size, Cass frowned. He looked like a small pony, and he ate like one, too. Maybe she'd better look for a diner job right away.

41

She'd better mention him in her first letter, as well. If her potential spouse hated dogs or was allergic to them, she needed to know up front.

She mentally began to compose her missive. Dear Mr. Maybe: Do you like ugly dogs? The thought of possible reactions to that opener made her smile.

Come live with me and be my love... Cass felt a pang of yearning at the romantic poem's request.

Did he like children? She'd better remember to ask. His ad hadn't said one way or the other. More and more couples were choosing not to have children these days, or putting it off until much later than she wanted to consider. She really didn't think she'd want to deal with two a.m. feedings at forty, for instance, even if diminished fertility wasn't an issue.

What else? He hadn't said what kind of business he had. Maybe he ran a salmon cannery. Would that affect her decision?

Cass mulled it over and decided it wouldn't thrill her, but if he was wonderful, she could tolerate fish odors for the rest of her life.

Wonderful made up for an awful lot. Committed made up for even more. And he sounded fairly stable, too. And romantic.

He sounded too good to be true, but Cass was just desperate enough to hope that sometimes dreams did come true. And she was certainly due for a lucky break.

He might just be the man of her dreams.

The man who'd win her heart, and give her his.

There was only one way to find out.

Chapter Three

I'm not much for poetry...

Oh, sure, Jason derided. According to Sam, that was far from true. Miss Lonely Hearts lied from the start. Her email had appeared promptly in response to his ad, her location marked as Seattle in the single's registration listing. And the clincher, her email had come with the drop-dead blonde photograph Sam described attached. Eyes like lapis lazuli, he'd said. And that much was true, although Jason didn't believe for a minute the lovely eyes in question belonged to his con artist.

The sweet face couldn't possibly belong to Miss Lonely Hearts, either. She'd stolen the face, the eyes and probably also the lyrical lure she'd used on Sam.

Jason ground his teeth and read on.

But I wouldn't mind if you wanted to read it to me.

Oh, she was smooth.

I'm reasonably attractive, single, female, blonde and very willing to relocate. Alaska sounds lovely. It also sounds very remote on your island.

Yes, it was her all right. She'd probably read reams on the island solitude from the Lawrence brothers and Sam. His ad certainly hadn't mentioned it, and Ketchikan wasn't a big spot on the map. If she knew something about his little adopted city, it had to be her.

Jason chuckled. This was really too easy. She'd taken the bait, and from the eager note of her email, she sounded ready to spring the trap on herself the moment he replied.

I'm interested in marriage, and I love children. Your ad didn't say, but I hope you feel the same. Children are definitely part of marriage for me.

He shook his head, laughing out loud now. What a line. She loved children. Sure, a knockout like that wanted to stretch her waistline and experience the joys of morning sickness? Not likely. It was part of the game. She was playing on his heartstrings.

Jason sobered as, unbidden, an image of the sweet-faced beauty, glowing with health and rounded in pregnancy, sprang to mind. He cursed under his breath. She knew what she was doing, all right. She was playing up to his masculine fantasies. Fantasies he hadn't even known he'd harbored in any corner of his mind.

I'm a freelance photographer and I love animals. Although I live in a big city now, I prefer rural life.

She might as well say she wanted to come and live in his kitchen, barefoot and pregnant. In the middle of nowhere. A beautiful woman like her.

Miss Lonely Hearts was downright treacherous. No wonder the Lawrence brothers had fallen under her spell. No wonder even cynical Sam hadn't been able to resist.

Her spiel was guaranteed to appeal directly to the masculine ego, feed and stroke it to maximum size, and then bleed the masculine wallet dry while the deluded victim thanked her for the pleasure of being robbed by her.

Jason might have been sorely tempted to drag her forcibly back and make her live up to her word if he thought there was even the remotest chance she looked anything like the photograph in his hand. Or that she had the sweet nature implied by her letter

Now there was a fantasy. A beautiful, sweet-natured woman, in love with him, happily raising children with him, turning his suite of rooms above the bar into a home.

Exactly what a solitary man craved most.

Jason hated her.

He was going to enjoy bringing her down, he really was.

I hope you like animals. I have a large dog of unknown parentage, and I couldn't give him up. He's very friendly and well trained.

Jason vacillated between fury and laughter. So now she claimed she loved animals. She even invented a fictitious mutt.

No woman who looked like the one in the enclosed picture would be caught dead walking a mutt. A pedigreed poodle, maybe. But a large mutt? Never. This was another ploy, cleverly designed to make her appear artless and genuine. What man wouldn't trust a dog lover?

Jason didn't know whether to be entertained or infuriated. He shook his head and read on.

I hope you'll reply soon and send me a picture of yourself. I'm looking forward to getting to know you better. Sincerely yours, Cassandra Adams.

Sincerely his? Jason sincerely doubted it. He doubted she'd been sincere about anything, ever.

He sincerely hoped she'd go directly for the money. He didn't think he could stand a drawn-out email correspondence with her. He'd underestimated her. She was a professional. If he gave her the opportunity, she'd have him tied up in knots and crying in his seltzer right next to Sam, Dwight and Duke.

Three weeks later, Cass opened the most recent message from her Alaskan man of mystery. Alex Sanders. Maybe today she'd finally get to put a face with the name. So far, he'd ducked her requests for a photo, making her wonder what he was hiding.

Dear Cass:

Every time I get another message from you, I find myself thinking this is too good to be true. But I do believe in miracles, my Cass, so I'll thank heaven for sending you my way.

Cass frowned. Was that a kind of backhanded compliment? She thought she detected a note of sarcasm there. She hesitated, then shrugged. He probably wasn't any better at writing than she was. Getting to know each other long-distance was bound to be awkward for both of them. They didn't have the advantage of facial expressions, tone of voice, or any of the subtle cues that helped give the written words context.

I'm attaching my picture for you since you keep asking for it. I hope you aren't disappointed. My own face doesn't compare to yours, but we can always hope the children take after you.

Eyebrows raised, Cass clicked on the attachment to see the photograph.

And didn't know what to think.

No, maybe she did. She thought he looked an awful lot like Rex. Appealing in a strange and homely way. Still, he did have nice eyes. And if he was anywhere near the devoted companion her mutt was, he measured pretty high on the husband desirability scale.

Tom had been stunningly handsome. Matthew even more so, she reminded herself.

Still, Cass admitted to a vain, shallow disappointment.

I'm certain any children you have will inherit your loveliness and make any man proud. I would like to be that man, Cass. I know it's sudden, but I've been given the chance of a lifetime, and I don't want to let it pass.

Marry me. Come to Alaska to meet me, and stay. I'll understand if you feel I'm rushing you, but please consider it. I'll be happy to pay your airfare.

And don't worry about your dog. I like animals. I'm sure I'll like yours.

I'm looking forward to your answer. Yours, Alex Sanders.

Cass sat back and thought it over. They'd established a rapport easily, and emails had shot back and forth at an increasingly rapid pace. She'd contacted several other candidates, too, not wanting to pin all her hopes on one possibility. But the tone of their emails, sometimes little cues, sometimes blatant, had eliminated all the others. None had been as interested or as interesting as Alex. Now he was proposing. And wanted to meet her in person.

Mrs. Sanders, she mused, turning the name over in her mind. Cassandra Sanders. A little repetitive, but then, she couldn't quibble over an unfortunate last name.

Knowing each other by email for the past few weeks did lead to a certain level of comfort and familiarity. Still, she knew that could be deceptive. Alex could be maintaining a façade online. But it wasn't as if they hadn't started out with the understanding that marriage was what they were both looking for. And maybe he had his reasons not to waste time. She certainly had hers.

Three million of them. On top of which her biological clock was ticking, reminding her she didn't have forever. She had no desire to go back to the dating jungle, even without her looming birthday deadline.

But was she ready to meet Alex in person? And how was she going to get there?

She was still waiting on payment from her last two freelance photography assignments, and she hadn't been able to find a new day job. She'd die before she'd go crawling back to her former boss. He might enjoy it, but he wouldn't rehire her, Cass knew. She wasn't about to give him the satisfaction of turning her down. On all fronts, it was as if the universe was conspiring against her to force her to make drastic life changes.

So, her proposed husband wanted an answer. Did she know enough to give him one yet?

She knew he was worlds above any of the other possibilities advertising in the singles pages. Some of the ones she'd written to had sounded barely literate, let alone compatible. She knew he wanted children. He didn't mind her dog. From his first message to this last, he sounded like the perfect, devoted husband. Was she going to hesitate over going to meet him because he was a stranger?

He'd still be a stranger after a hundred emails, on one level. Some things she'd never know until she actually met him in person. Like whether or not they had chemistry. Even if they switched from email to chat, she couldn't get a real feel for the physical side of things.

Alex wanted to meet her. He wanted to marry her. And in spite of his homely face, she wanted to meet him. He wasn't ugly. He did have a certain appeal. And something in his emails made her wonder if there wasn't really something there. Something she'd regret not taking a chance on if she talked herself out of not moving forward now.

Think of it as an interview with a prospective client, she told herself. If you don't click, you can always say no and walk away. But maybe you won't want to. Maybe he's just what you want.

Cass wavered. Her eyes swept around the apartment and fell on Rex. She didn't have any other prospects on the horizon. She didn't want to give up her inheritance without a fight. And she didn't really want to spend the next ten years living with a dog as her sole companion, either. No matter what happened with Alex, she needed to act. She realized the real reason for her hesitation was the worry that they wouldn't click, and she'd started to count on him as her solution a little too much.

She looked forward to his emails. They made her smile, sometimes made her shake her head, and often seemed like something was slipping past her, but overall, contact with Alex made her feel good.

She *could* go. She could meet him and see if there was something there worth pursuing or not. There was just one small problem.

Until she got paid for her freelance work, she didn't have the extra money for airfare to Alaska for one passenger and one dog, and the Alaska ferry was even more expensive than flying from Sea-Tac. No telling when the payment would show up, either.

He'd offered to pay for her ticket, she reminded herself. She'd be able to pay him back as soon as her checks arrived, and once all the legalities were settled, she'd be able to draw on her trust and money wouldn't be a worry at all.

And possibly due to the universal conspiracy that seemed to be at work in her life, she'd just been offered a photography job in Ketchikan for the summer. All she had to do was get there, and Alex had just offered her the means.

Still, it felt very uncomfortable. It meant she'd be depending on somebody other than herself. For a small thing, sure, but marriage meant depending on each other for all kinds of things.

Much bigger things than plane tickets.

Maybe she really wasn't ready for this. The thought sank in, and Cass felt suddenly vulnerable.

Then she took a breath and squared her shoulders. For her parents, and many other couples, marriage worked just fine. Yes, there were plenty of failures, but how much of that came from picking the wrong person in the first place?

She was letting nerves affect her, but there was nothing to be nervous about in just going to meet him. And she had no reason to think Alex would be undependable. Just the opposite, in fact. He sounded eager to take on the responsibilities of not only a wife, but children and one large dog.

She really couldn't ask for more. He sounded like the epitome of the committed family man she wanted. She was being offered a chance. One she really couldn't afford to pass up.

Her decision firm, Cass opened a reply window and prepared to drastically alter the course of her life. She hoped it wasn't a mistake. But if it was, she'd deal with it, and she'd be just fine. Like always. And no matter what happened, at least she'd be out of the rain.

Dear Alex:

Thank you for your letter and picture. Like you, I find myself thinking this must be too good to be true. Family men are rare these days, at least in Seattle.

Alex, I'd be happy to accept your proposal if you're anywhere near as wonderful in person as you are in email. I'd love to meet you. Unfortunately, I'm between jobs and to be honest, I don't have the resources to fly out.

Ah, there it was. Miss Lonely Hearts had just taken the bait and swallowed the hook. Jason gave a wicked laugh. He had her now.

If you don't mind sending a ticket for myself and my dog, I'd be delighted to come.

This is sort of an awkward way to say 'yes', isn't it? Maybe we can do better in person. I'll be watching for your reply. Cass.

Yes, it was going to be very interesting when they met in person. But not the way she thought. She didn't think they'd be meeting at all. Jason smiled in anticipation, thinking of the surprise and chagrin on his nemesis' face when he unmasked her.

He thought he'd been particularly clever in using a false name and picture, in case it was someone he knew. If she thought he was on to her, she'd probably disappear instead of springing his trap.

It was worth a flight to Seattle for the fun of catching the con artist who'd dared to poach on his territory. Jason's wicked smile broadened. He'd catch her in the act of stealing, and he'd make her pay.

"Heard you were making some progress, Jason," Sam remarked as he settled on a stool.

Jason nodded, smiling evilly. "Oh, yes. Miss Lonely Hearts has outsmarted herself. And get this, she's upped the take. She wants airfare for her fictitious dog, too." He poured Sam's usual libation as he spoke and placed the drink on a cocktail napkin before him.

"Thanks. So it's her, and she's raised the price? Interesting."

Interesting was not the word for it. Jason was going to enjoy breaking her larcenous little heart in retaliation for the damage she'd done. She'd gone beyond targeting The Last Resort. It was personal now. Because in spite of everything, even knowing what she was, she'd gotten to him.

Unbelievable, but there it was. With every lying word she wrote, he found himself wishing she was telling the truth, and knowing she'd hooked him infuriated him. He'd played his part well, but even while he was playing her, he knew she'd managed to play him. If he hadn't known what she was in advance, he'd be her current victim. Interesting was certainly one word for that.

"Yes, isn't it," he agreed with Sam in a neutral voice.

Dwight and Duke arrived for their evening ritual and Jason busied himself pouring and serving, but he was too distracted to fully enjoy their silent pantomime performance.

"You got the picture?" Sam asked him when he finished.

Jason nodded. He had it in his wallet, where he'd been keeping it for the past few weeks. Not because it meant anything, he told himself, but because it kept him in the proper frame of mind for revenge. He took it out and placed it in front of Dwight like a dealer laying down an ace and polished an imaginary mark on the bar.

If he'd been paying attention, he might have noticed a stiffness in Dwight's shoulders before he passed the picture to Duke. The two exchanged a look. Then Dwight slid the picture back to him, face down with a clap on the arm.

"Mind if I see?" Sam made the mild request after watching the byplay between the untalkative twosome.

"No." Jason handed the picture over and continued buffing the already spotless bar with deliberate concentration.

Sam studied the photograph for a moment, then glanced at the Lawrence twins. He could have sworn he read a silent warning in their eyes. "Yes, that's a face no man would forget," he mused, handing it back.

Jason took it and stuffed it back into his wallet without looking at it. "I'm sure that was the idea," he snarled.

"Yes. Well. So, you're sending the tickets?"

"Oh, yes. And I'm going to Seattle to keep an eye on the ticket counter personally. When she shows up to trade them in, I'm going to bust her." Satisfaction oozed from him, and Sam exchanged another look with the Lawrences.

"Good plan." He sipped at his drink for a moment. "Still, I hope you won't be too hard on her."

Jason slapped his towel on the bar and stared at Sam, incredulous. "Don't be too hard on her?"

Sam cleared his throat uneasily. "Well, you know, an engagement does leave certain feelings." He hoped the Lawrences would help, but he couldn't see how.

Jason swung to look at the twins. "You, too? You're all still soft on her?"

The two big men shuffled their feet, looked at each other, and then looked at their shots of bourbon, which they proceeded to down in unison.

"Incredible," Jason stated. "You'd actually let her get away with it, wouldn't you? Don't you realize what you're dealing with here? She's not a nice girl. She preys on men. She plays up to their fantasies and messes with their minds. Outright robbery would be kinder, but she steals more than money. She's out to steal souls."

He didn't seem to notice his diatribe was rather emotional for a calm, uninvolved arbiter of justice.

"Well," Sam murmured apologetically, "a man can't help his feelings, can he? I hope you'll go easy on her, that's all."

Jason's face lost all expression before he turned to pour

himself a seltzer. "No. A man can't help his feelings."

Dwight frowned at Sam as if to say *I told you so*. Sam nodded.

He wouldn't tell, and they wouldn't, either. Still, it was rather touching, even to a confirmed cynic. Their bartender was going to go get himself a mail-order bride. He hadn't caught Miss Lonely Hearts, but it seemed he'd definitely caught his woman. Sam just hoped the sweet little thing wouldn't kill her groom when she found out she'd been married under false pretenses. That there would be a wedding was a foregone conclusion, judging by Jason's reaction.

Sam also hoped she wouldn't find out about his own part in the affair. She did have a rather stubborn chin, and those pretty eyes could probably turn downright mean.

"Are you really sure about this, Cass?" Lisa's worried eyes searched hers, and Cass smiled reassuringly.

"No."

"Great." Lisa threw her hands up and sat on the bed amid suitcases and boxes. "You're not sure about this, but you're going to do it anyway."

"Yep." Cass smiled at her friend as she closed another bag.

Lisa drummed on a convenient box as she considered the calm blonde. "So then, why are you doing it?"

Cass gave her her full attention. "How many reasons do you want? The money? The fact that I'd rather marry my dog than see Tom indirectly benefit from my inheritance after dumping me to marry my cousin? The looming deadline? Besides, I was sure about Matthew. I was sure about Tom. Look how being sure turned out."

Lisa frowned.

A distraction was in order, Cass decided. "Anyway, I've got a job with a fishing charter company photographing tourists with their prize salmon for the summer. I'm broke now, but I won't be as soon as I start shooting. And I'll have free time to do stock shots of the scenery. I can probably do some work for local businesses and the chamber of commerce, too. It's a good career move. Speaking of careers, how'd your tryout with the Sirens go? Or haven't you gone yet?"

It worked. Lisa sat upright and beamed. "It's tonight. I've been practicing to their album. The rhythms are wonderfully complex. I can't wait." Her enthusiasm carried over into an airy display of a triumphant high-hat hit, and Cass laughed.

"You'll be great, I know it. Help me close this suitcase, would you?"

Lisa moved to assist her and slanted her a wry look. "You wouldn't be trying to distract me, would you?"

Cass blinked. "Me?"

"Yeah, you. All right, I give up." Lisa waved her arms in surrender. "It's your life, and you're an adult. Go marry a stranger. And who knows, he may turn out to be your Prince Charming. Even if he turns out to be a frog, it beats losing to your rotten relatives."

"I'm meeting him first, remember? If he's a jerk, or kicks my dog, or does anything I don't like, I'll call it off. I'm not doing anything irreversible, you know," Cass pointed out. "Besides, every day I hate Seattle more. I'd be moving anyway. And I think Alaska might really suit me. There's something about it. Just think of all the natural beauty I could photograph."

"I know. You're right. You're doing the right thing and it's not like there's really any choice. I'm just going to miss you."

Cass bit her lip and fought sudden tears. "I'll miss you, too."

They hugged and sniffled for a moment, then laughed at their own sentimentalism.

"Look at us. The wedding march isn't even playing, and we're crying," Lisa groused.

"Well, since you won't be there, we had to get it out of the way before I left."

The two friends grinned at each other.

"So, you're off to Alaska to become a mail-order bride. I'm sure anything that sounds so romantic can't be all bad." Lisa was plainly trying to work up some enthusiasm for the idea, and Cass laughed again, feeling lighter every moment.

"Lisa, everything will be fine. I'm looking forward to this. I need a change, and this is a big one. And maybe Rex will find a nice wolf or something." She grinned at the thought of her mutt pursuing a wolf, who would probably be too amazed at his audacity to run away.

"What a thought. Can you imagine the poor puppies?" Lisa groaned.

"Puppies are always cute. They'd make him look handsome by comparison." Cass giggled. "Although since he's fixed, we'll never know what his offspring would've looked like."

"Speaking of handsome, are you going to tell me what your mystery man looks like?"

Suddenly serious, Cass answered, "He's perfect." He was. The last thing she wanted was another handsome, untrustworthy, unreliable lowlife.

Alex wasn't handsome, but she was fairly certain he'd be loyal. And they wanted the same things. That made him perfect for her. On top of that, she had a feeling that wouldn't go away that there was something about him. Something that compelled her to go and see if maybe, just maybe there was something real between them or if the connection she felt through email was all in her head.

"Well, I don't know why I'm trying to talk you out of this." Lisa scooped up a box and followed Cass out to the piles of storage items versus travel items. "The way supposedly based on love marriages are turning out, you'll probably be happily married fifty years from now while the rest of us are in divorce court."

"That's my plan," Cass agreed. "Not for you to end up divorced, but for me to stay married."

Lisa grinned. "I assumed that."

Between the two of them, it didn't take long to pack away the items Cass wanted to leave stored, and get the rest loaded into Lisa's car for the drive to the airport.

"Okay, do you have everything?"

Cass wrinkled her nose. "Yes, Mom. I have my ID, my plane ticket, all that stuff. And the doggie dope."

Lisa eyed Rex's oversized shape, and then glanced back at Cass. "You're not going to dope him now?"

"No, we'd never carry him. I'll do it there, and he'll sleep through the trip peacefully." At least, the vet had promised he would. He wasn't a good flier. The one other time she'd flown with him, he'd made an unholy racket and managed to get loose from his travel cage. Cass hoped he'd do better this time.

"Well, I guess this is it then."

Cass nodded and took a final look around her old home. Then she signaled her dog to come and locked the door for the last time, handing Lisa the key.

All too soon, Rex was on his way to the pet section, asleep

as promised, and the two women piled the luggage on the carousel.

"Let's hope my luggage and I go to the same destination," Cass muttered.

"Oh, now you're pessimistic?"

"Yeah, I think the odds that I'm about to meet and marry a good guy are far better than the odds on my luggage not going to Singapore."

Lisa laughed at the dark tone. "Well, if that's the case, you'll have a really interesting honeymoon."

With no clothes? Yes, she had a point. Cass smiled in response.

They made their way to the right section and dropped into chairs just before the security checkpoint, where they'd have to separate.

"So, this is it," the drummer sighed. "You're leaving."

"Yes. And I expect an autograph from you after tonight," Cass reminded her. "You're about to be famous."

"Done. I'll call you as soon as I know. You have this mystery man's phone number, don't you?"

"No." Cass said, surprised to realize she didn't. "I should have asked. There were so many other details, I just never thought about it. It must be in the directory, though. Anyway, it's probably better if I call you."

Lisa nodded. "Okay."

"Okay."

They exchanged looks, knowing they were putting off the inevitable. Then Lisa hugged her and stood. "All right, I'm going. I just have time now to get back, change and get to my audition."

"Good luck," Cass offered.

"You, too."

After a final hug, Cass sat back down, alone, and watched her friend walk away. Lisa turned once to wave, and she waved back. Then she was really alone, ready to go through the security check, head to her gate and wait for the plane.

She was really doing this. Was she nuts? She hoped not. She really hoped not.

Jason watched the tall blonde with a growing sense of disbelief. The last thing he'd expected was to find Miss Lonely Hearts using her own face. Or using his ticket. She was in line, and when the boarding call came, she got on.

Now what? He had the seat next to hers. He knew, because he'd bought the two tickets together, but he'd never expected hers to get used.

Jason glanced at the time. Fifteen minutes, at least. He had time to make a phone call before he went to meet his mail-order bride. And he knew just who he was going to call.

He pulled out his cell phone, tapped out a number and waited.

"Last Resort."

"Sam, I think you owe me an explanation."

"Now, Jason, don't go losing your temper," Sam cautioned.

"I am not losing my temper," Jason bit out. "I am perfectly calm, and I want an explanation."

"Well, you got the wrong woman." Sam harrumphed. "Only I thought maybe you had the right one, after all. So I didn't think your trip to Seattle was such a bad idea."

Great. His customers, even Dwight and Duke, were playing matchmaker. Miss Lonely Hearts was still running around loose, and he now had an unexpected bride to deal with. And her dog. If she was real, he had to assume the oversized mutt of indeterminate parentage was, too. Jason resisted the urge to pound his head against the nearest wall with remarkable restraint.

"So you sent me here to get married?" he demanded.

Sam coughed. "Ah, well. Well, if you are going to marry her, the preacher's waiting. Here, that is. Or you could just tell her the truth and send her home before the plane takes off."

"Right."

"Of course, it sounds like she could use a man who'd look out for her. Seems a shame to leave her all alone in a big city."

Now that was a direct hit to his protective instincts. Sam was as good at manipulation as Miss Lonely Hearts.

"And it seemed to me, the way you kept carrying around her emails and her picture, maybe there was something there."

Her emails. Her face. They'd gotten under his skin. Gotten him thinking. Wanting. In spite of everything he'd thought he knew about her.

Yes, there was something there. So what was he going to do about it?

Jason thought through his alternatives, and then consulted his gambler's instincts. Gamblers were notoriously unlucky at love. But he knew as well as Sam did there was going to be a wedding anyway.

As part of his possibly insane plan to bring Miss Lonely Hearts to justice, he'd already dealt with the marriage license registration and had been sure he'd had her when she didn't balk at that step. What the hell had he been thinking, taking it that far?

That he wanted her, dammit. That he wanted her to be for real. There was no other explanation. And now he could have her, if he played his cards right.

"Have the bakery make a cake, okay?" Jason made the request in a distracted voice. He didn't have time to do much, and he had a feeling the more points he had in his favor tonight, the better the odds of his marriage surviving the sunrise would become.

"Sure, Jason."

"Okay. See you soon." Jason hung up, shook his head over the bizarre chain of events, and went to meet his wife-to-be.

Chapter Four

"Excuse me, I have the window seat."

Cass glanced up when a voice like whiskey that went down smooth and left a trail of fire behind intruded on her racing thoughts. Her eyes traveled over the snug jeans, up the equally close-fitting forest green polo shirt to the handsome face with whiskey-colored eyes to match the voice and brown hair streaked with amber and gold.

Just her luck. She had to get seated next to a handsome womanizer. She could tell he was a womanizer by the interested gleam in his eyes as they roamed up and down her before settling back on her face.

Wordlessly, Cass pulled her long legs in to let him step past and went back to reading the magazine she'd picked up for the flight.

"Thanks." He seated himself next to her and his thigh brushed hers. He couldn't help that, the seats were too close together, but a frisson of electricity from the point of contact startled her.

Cass shifted her weight to the opposite hip and crossed her legs to avoid further contact. This was an unexpected annoyance, and it just proved that she'd spent too many months having boring sex with Tom followed by no sex at all. If brushing against a stranger made her tingle, it was really time to fix her personal life. Which she was trying to do.

In the meantime, she could just stay in this position. It was a short flight. No more uncomfortable chills up her spine and a clear non-verbal signal to Whiskey Eyes that she didn't want to get to know him better.

He didn't take the hint.

"My name's Jason," the man announced in a warm voice. He held out a square hand to shake hers.

Out of habit, Cass shook it. Electricity again. Dancing over her skin and making hidden nerves sing. It distracted her and made her leave her hand in his too long.

Maybe the same charge was skittering over his skin because he didn't seem to notice the polite handshake was going on far too long. He didn't release her hand. Didn't seem to want to release her.

Since she was fighting the same bizarre urge to prolong the contact, irritation welled up. This she did not need. And it was coming from him so it was his fault, Cass decided. She glared at him as she exerted control over herself and attempted to tug free.

Finally, she snapped, "Let go of my hand."

He smiled, golden flecks dancing in his warm eyes. "Now that's a voice," he remarked. "You sound as good as you look. I was beginning to wonder, the way you seemed to be avoiding talking."

"Thank you. Now please let go of my hand." *Before I forget why I want you to.*

Jason did so, but seemed determined to hang onto the topic, if not her. "If you get scared during take-off, I can hold your hand again."

Cass smiled back at him, placing her hand safely in her

lap. "I love take-offs. And landing. Unless there's turbulence, it's the only interesting part of flying."

It was the wrong thing to say. His brows formed twin arcs and he looked intrigued. "Ah, you have a love of adventure and danger?"

No. She certainly didn't. Her career was risky enough. She was dedicating her personal life to playing it safe. Which included marrying a safe man, instead of one who was danger personified. Like him. Cass chose to ignore his leading remark and instead turned the page, although she hadn't read a word of the article.

Jason, apparently not burdened by politeness, leaned over her shoulder to read with her. "How to Re-grout Your Tile?"

She narrowed her eyes as they made scorching contact with his golden ones. Unperturbed, they glowed with warmth and humor. "Now, that doesn't sound at all dangerous," he teased.

Cass smiled. "Exactly."

"Exactly?" Mr. Charm settled into the corner, putting his back to the window view to fix his disturbing eyes more easily on her. "Now that sounds like a story."

The story of her life. Cass wasn't about to tell it to him, either. She looked around the small plane and wondered if she could move once they were in the air. It wasn't full yet. There might be empty seats.

Just her bad luck, she had to get seated next to a man like him on her way to meet the man she was going to marry. She knew his type. It was the type she fell for. The type she'd sworn off. The type she was going to avoid.

Because his type wasn't interested in settling down or putting in the effort it would take to make a relationship last.

His was also the type that wasn't easily discouraged, it seemed, as he launched into a monologue. "I can't help wondering why a beautiful woman with a taste for danger wants to read about grout. It makes me even more curious when she doesn't want to talk to a stranger. It makes me wonder if she's afraid."

Cass swung towards him. "I am not afraid. I'm not afraid of anything."

Too late, she realized her reaction was exactly what he'd been hoping for. He'd baited her, and she'd leaped for it like a prize trout. His eyes glowed with satisfaction and he leaned forward in interest.

"Now, you see, that's just what I mean," he stated, giving her a warm smile. "You're a little too quick to say that. It makes me wonder why you're so touchy on the subject."

Cass wondered when the Fasten Seatbelts light would come on, with the usual safety spiel. Maybe the distraction would derail her seatmate and he'd move on to something else. Like sleeping. Or drinking.

If she had to keep listening to him, *she'd* be drinking to blot out the fact that his whiskey eyes and his whiskey voice and the electric effect he had on her were making her feel tipsy even though she was stone sober.

"Take this flight, for example."

Cass pretended to ignore him and refused to answer.

Undeterred, the stranger continued, "Going to Alaska, now that's an adventure. The Last Frontier, and so on. Glaciers, Eskimos, although actually we have Innuits in Alaska and there aren't any igloos. But still, it's an adventure."

She wasn't going to answer. She absolutely wasn't. Cass fixed her eyes on a diagram showing grout repair in corners and around faucet fixtures.

"Now, the thing about Alaska, it's sort of an extension of the Old West. People went west to start over."

She gave an involuntary start and glanced his way. His eyes gleamed with humor and satisfaction as they met hers.

"People who might be running from something. Bad decisions or bad memories, for example."

Cass fixed her eyes back on her magazine and stared down at the article again. He couldn't know. He couldn't possibly. He was taking shots in the dark and he'd gotten lucky. Besides, she wasn't running from, she was moving to. The past was over and done with but she had no intention of giving up on her future.

"Or people with a bad case of over-the-ridge, far horizons syndrome. People with wanderlust. Itchy feet."

That would be him, Cass thought. Itchy feet and wanderlust. Exactly why she'd vowed to avoid his type in her new life. One day he'd decide to wander off, leaving a wife and a baby and a toddler to cope alone.

After Matthew, she was no longer naive enough to believe all this man needed was the right woman to convince him to settle down. That way led to heartbreak, and she was determined to keep her heart in one piece from now on.

"People on their way to new jobs," the man went on in a cheerful tone. "I missed all the pipeline excitement, but it brought in all kinds and many of them stayed on."

Cass vaguely remembered the hoopla about the Alaskan Pipeline, although she'd been a little young and more interested in things more immediately important to her world.

"And of course, Alaska gets a few mail-order brides."

Her hands were not shaking, Cass promised herself. She was being overly sensitive. She was a little nervous about meeting Alex, that was all. The man next to her was not making her doubt the wisdom of her decision.

"That's a real adventure," he continued. "Marriage. That's the big leap into the unknown."

Cass didn't respond and pretended a deep and abiding interest in grout care.

"Can you imagine the kind of nerve it would take for a woman to agree to marry a total stranger and leave everything she knows?" Jason went on in a musing tone. "Marriage is risky enough with someone you know, don't you agree?"

"Yes," she answered with feeling. Right away she regretted it. He was going to pounce on the opening.

He did. "That sounds like the voice of experience. Are you married?"

"Engaged." Sort of. The flat response should discourage him. But Cass was beginning to think nothing short of a tranquilizer dart would accomplish that goal. He was charming and determined and far too damned attractive. He undoubtedly knew it and was used to playing on his strengths. Seducing women just because he could was probably some sort of hobby for him.

Too bad he was obviously really good at it.

His eyes gleamed. "Interesting. And who's the lucky man you're engaged to? He must be quite a guy."

"He is." She hoped.

"Known him long?"

"No."

"No?" The man looked thoughtful.

Cass decided to discourage him further if he was thinking along the lines of hinting she hadn't known Alex long enough. "There's more to getting to know someone than how much time is involved."

She frowned slightly thinking of how long she'd known Matthew, and the shock of his betrayal. They'd been engaged for two years. How could he have lied to her the whole time? And Tom. She'd known him for months before they started dating. Another six months before he proposed. No, time had nothing to do with how well you knew someone. After all that time, they'd still been strangers in all the ways that really mattered. Considering her record, she was safer with a man she'd never met.

"Now, that's an interesting perspective," Jason observed. "So you think you know this man you're marrying well enough?"

Cass met his eyes with a level stare. "As well as anyone ever really knows anyone else. Well enough to know he's everything I've ever wanted in a husband. Well enough to know the important things." She willed it to be true even as she said it. Who was she trying to convince, herself, or this Jason?

He leaned forward, either intrigued or doing a good job of faking it. "Oh? And what is it that you consider important in a husband?"

She leaned back and settled into the headrest and gazed ahead. "Honesty."

For an endless minute, the word seemed to hang in the air between them.

"Honesty," Jason repeated.

She nodded. Then the Fasten Seatbelts light came on, and the flight attendant's safety spiel gave Cass an excuse to escape the conversation. She fixed her eyes on the arrows leading to the exits as if she believed the plane was going to go down and her life would depend on knowing where to find the nearest one.

Honesty. The word seemed to repeat itself to Jason in a

mocking echo. She considered honesty the most important thing? He was doomed. He was stuck playing for high stakes with a bum hand and now there was no alternative but to bluff his way through.

Lady Luck, smile on me one last time.

Not that Lady Luck was known for making any gambler lucky when it came to the ultimate play of hearts. That was the trouble with giving up the game and settling down, he mused. When you had nothing to lose, it was easy to keep a cool head, a blank expression and a steady hand. And the winnings kept coming. Then he'd decided he could allow himself to have a home outside of the world of casinos. Look what that led to. Pretty soon a home wasn't enough, because he was the only one in it. Then he started wanting what he couldn't have.

That was the real reason for his vendetta with Miss Lonely Hearts. The admission sank in gradually and Jason pondered it. He'd reacted the way he had because the whole subject exposed a raw nerve. Promises that were never kept. Love that never lasted. The warmth and belonging he yearned for but could never quite reach. And then he'd stopped reaching and told himself he'd be content with the only person he could count on—himself. But the longing hadn't gone away. He'd only succeeded in burying it so well that he'd hidden it even from himself, until he found a home in The Last Resort and started to imagine he could have a family to share it with.

He hadn't had a family since he was eight years old, when his mother died. A bitter, mostly absent father didn't count. He'd gone his own way as soon as he was able. A gift for memory, an ability with numbers, sure instincts and the peculiar confidence that came with having nothing to lose made him a natural gambler.

That, and the fact that he never drank. The casinos served

free drinks to patrons for a reason—to encourage them to loosen inhibitions and play on when the luck of the draw turned. Jason never lost due to impaired judgment from drinking. And he always knew when it was time to walk away, even when he was winning.

This time, there'd be no walking away. He'd known that before he'd brushed against her and felt his body come alive, seen the same reaction in her before she could hide it. Sam had been right, there was definitely something here. He wasn't about to walk away from it. So all he had to do was make certain he didn't lose.

He stole a glance at Cass. She was reading her magazine with deliberate concentration. Trying to ignore him and not succeeding. That made him smile inside. He studied the curve of her lower lip, the way she nibbled on it. A tell? A sign of agitation?

His gaze slid lower to the soft swell of feminine breasts, the indentation below her ribs and the corresponding rounding of her belly and hips. The graceful line of her long legs. Desire rushed through him with a force that took him by surprise. How long had it been? He couldn't remember the last time he'd wanted a woman.

Women weren't a part of his life. Relationships had belonged in the category of things a gambler had no right to. The only women he'd known were a series of distant partners who asked nothing and expected nothing and went their way afterwards, still strangers.

It was unsatisfying, and after a while, it hadn't seemed worth it for the momentary gratification. Then he'd made the change to settling down and running his business, and there hadn't been time. Or much opportunity. Sam had been right about that, the tourists passed through and the options for any permanent relationship were limited.

Now here sat this woman who invited him with her softness, her nearness. She had a quality of gentleness that made him ache. And if he played his cards right, she could be his wife before the day was over.

He threw caution to the winds. He'd marry her any way he could, and deal with the lies later. It wasn't as if he'd deliberately set out to deceive her. And she wanted a husband, didn't she? Why else would she answer an ad for a mail-order bride? She wanted him. And he wanted her.

Other marriages that lasted had been based on less. It wasn't a bad foundation to begin with. Maybe it wasn't the stuff of romantic daydreams, but she was evidently a practical woman. They could make it work. Well, they could if he could keep her from walking out on him and off the island when she found out she'd been lied to and he'd originally intended to trap her, not get married to her.

Jason turned that thought over. Maybe Sam had foreseen that difficulty and arranged something. If not, they could always work together to convince her she was stranded. Sam had it coming for his collusion with the Lawrences, anyway. He wasn't in this alone. They could at least back him up.

An old gambler's adage said you couldn't win if you didn't risk it. Now that he had something more important than money to lose, it was time to raise and call. He'd risk it. He'd hedge his bet as thoroughly as possible at the same time, but he was prepared to take the gamble that he could win the only time it really mattered.

Besides, it was entirely in keeping with the spirit of the Old West to win a wife in a gamble. He was just upholding a tradition. He was a traditional kind of man.

Settled, Jason made himself as comfortable as he could in

the cramped seat and enjoyed the scenery with his back to the window. His wife-to-be was worth watching, even when she was trying to ignore him and pretending a fascination with the mysteries of tile grout.

Even if she really was fascinated with tile grout, it might not be a bad thing. The Last Resort had some that could use the attention of an enthusiastic expert.

In fact, the more he considered it the more the idea of a partner appealed to him. The Last Resort had once been a bordello and he'd never gotten around to doing much with the upstairs rooms, besides the section he lived in. He'd had vague plans to expand into renting rooms to tourists, maybe starting a limited menu at the bar. Maybe a wife could help with the project.

Maybe she'd have some ideas about the hospitality business. Her emails had indicated that she'd done a lot of restaurant work. Her talents were bound to come in handy, as long as she didn't want to paint everything pink. The Last Resort was a man's bar and always had been. It had started out as a gentleman's refuge, and the ladies who'd lived there had catered to masculine preferences. Whatever ideas she had would have to go along with the traditional oak, brass and leather decor. Jason would be firm with her about that.

He was staring at her.

Cass stared at her magazine with unseeing eyes and tried not to look self-conscious.

He was staring at her. Why was he staring at her?

Because you shook his hand and then held it and acted like a teenager with a crush. Way to go, Cass. Maybe he thought she was interested in him. Maybe he thought she was easy. Maybe he thought she was lying about being engaged. Although she sort of was. Maybe. That part hadn't been too clear, now that she thought about it. Were they actually engaged?

Her mind was racing and she hauled it back with an effort. It didn't matter what some stranger on a plane thought, she told herself.

Right.

She slammed the magazine shut and turned to face him. "Why are you staring at me?"

He gave her an innocent look. "Staring? Was I staring?"

"Yes." She frowned at him. "It's rude."

He smiled, fairly oozing charm. "Forgive me. It isn't every day I find myself next to such a lovely woman."

Cass nodded. "I'm sure. They must get up and leave due to your rudeness."

Jason gave her a wounded look.

"Stop that. You know you're being rude. I think you're doing it on purpose. You're trying to make me nervous, aren't you? Well, it isn't going to work." She faced forward once more and started to read.

He lifted the magazine from her grasp, turned it right side up and returned it to her.

She wasn't going to say anything. He'd better not say anything either, Cass decided.

He didn't.

But when she looked, he was smirking. Positively smirking. Laughter danced in his eyes and the knowing expression on his face made her long to roll up the magazine and bring it down on his thick head.

It was tempting.

As if he saw the idea forming, he held up his hands to ward

her off. "I was only trying to help."

She glared. Then she turned her attention back to her reading and fixed her eyes on the page as if her life depended on learning everything there was to know about preventing mildew.

"I mean it," Jason went on. "The importance of grout care is often overlooked. Neglect it, and you pay the price. I think I'm going to have to completely replace mine. Lucky Day didn't know the first thing about preventing mildew build-up."

"Lucky Day?" The startled question slipped out in spite of herself, and the man took it as encouragement.

"The former owner of The Last Resort. It's a bar and potential hotel, but it needs work. I won it from him in a poker game two years ago."

Won it? In a poker game? She'd known it, she'd just known it. He was a gambler. A drifter. Unreliable. She sniffed and turned the page. His grout troubles didn't interest her in the least.

"You don't approve of gambling?" The amused question in that lazy, whiskey-smooth voice told her that he knew very well that she disapproved strongly. "Well, I admit it isn't for everyone."

His tone implied that the world was big enough for the adventurous to allow a little room for the clean-the-grout types.

Cass stiffened in silent offense.

"You're upset. Does it bother you to be sitting next to a gambler?" Jason rubbed his chin in absent musing. "I'll bet it does."

She sighed and turned to meet his laughing eyes. "That's a terrible joke. If you tell jokes like that to your customers, it's a miracle you have any."

"But you want to laugh," he pointed out, assured charm

gleaming in the depths of his eyes. "Admit it. You want to disapprove, but you can't help yourself. You like me."

"I do not. I don't know you well enough to like or dislike you." And she wasn't ever going to either, Cass finished silently. She was going to marry a man who looked like her dog and live happily ever after, taking art photographs of her family over the years in between paying assignments.

"Yes, you do." He sat back and hooked one ankle over the opposite knee. "Tell me about this paragon you're marrying. Is he good looking?"

Beauty was in the eye of the beholder, Cass decided. "Yes."

"Really." Undisguised disbelief denounced her as a liar.

"Really." She smiled wider, enjoying turning the tables on him. Then she realized sparring with him verbally was that damn unwanted electricity taking on another form. She felt charged and alive. That wasn't right.

Jason wondered if love really was blind. She thought she was marrying a good-looking man? Had she actually taken a good look at that photograph?

He'd found the worst picture of the homeliest man in town to send to her. He'd done it while inwardly laughing at Miss Lonely Hearts and her sinking stomach, imagining her horrified reaction.

Mason hadn't minded when he borrowed his picture. Mason didn't mind much of anything anyone took it into their heads to do. As long as they minded the rules and didn't leave garbage in the woods or start forest fires, Mason Evan was a happy forestry service employee.

The man in the picture he'd sent her looked like an unshaven, untamed mountain man. Which, basically, he was. And she liked him? She was actually willing to marry him?

Jason was in big trouble.

"Besides," she went on, "I didn't like Seattle."

"Oh?"

She nodded. "It rains all the time. I hate rain."

Jason's eyes widened in horrified realization. Then he started to choke.

Cass immediately waved for the flight attendant. "Could I get a glass of water for this man?"

"Sure thing." With a sympathetic look, the woman hurried to fill a cup and delivered it.

"Thank you." She turned and pressed it into Jason's hand. "Here, drink this."

"No. No, really. I'm fine." He waved her away and wiped at his streaming eyes.

"I don't think you are." Concern knit her brows together and she nibbled at her lower lip again. "Please drink the water."

Jason met her eyes and wanted to groan. He was lost.

She was beautiful. She loved animals. She loved children. She was willing to give even a man who looked like Mountain Man Mason a chance. She made the air around him crackle. And she was kind to strangers, too.

Unable to deny her anything, Jason took the water and drank it.

"There," she said, sounding satisfied. "Doesn't that help?"

No. Nothing was going to help, he wanted to tell her. But she wasn't going to hear it from him. At least, not yet. Not now, when she could so easily walk away forever, before they'd even had a chance.

"Yes," he lied. He was doing it so much now, he was getting good at it.

If this kept up, his nose was going to grow.

Jason wondered if Mason was going to be in town. He hadn't even considered the possibility before, but it could be a real problem now. Mason might be a bit slow, but no man could be fool enough to turn down this woman and leave her standing at the altar.

No, he'd go quietly along with her even if he hadn't ever heard of her or her letters before and he'd be saying "I do" in his sonorous voice before Jason could say "I object!"

He'd have to convince her that her fiancé was unavoidably detained and that they'd marry by proxy. He'd be the stand-in. That would work. Wouldn't it? Damn. Where was Sam and his interfering plotting when he was needed?

His racing thoughts were interrupted by the object of his rapidly growing obsession.

"You don't look very well. Do you want to sit by the aisle?"

The soft sympathy made him feel like the lowest criminal.

"No, I'm fine," he lied again.

It was getting easier.

Chapter Five

Cass found her first view of Ketchikan something of a disappointment. The airplane offered a pretty good view, but one thing spoiled it.

It was raining.

That didn't strike her as a particularly good omen. Especially considering why she was there. Wasn't there some kind of bad luck associated with weddings and rainy days?

She shifted the bag she'd carried, now holding the magazine she hadn't read more than one sentence of, and nibbled her lower lip in vague apprehension.

Rain wasn't a good sign.

Maybe this whole mail-order marriage was a bad plan.

Then she straightened in determination. She was being ridiculous. So it was raining. What was she, a superstitious idiot? No. Of course not. She was sensible, damn it. Practical. A serious, sensible, practical woman making a thoroughly thought-out decision and she wasn't going to be put off by a little rain. Not any more than she'd be put off by a too-handsome gambler who sparked her nerve endings with the slightest contact and made her want to argue with him because it was fun.

Still, she found herself wistfully wishing the sun would

peek through the clouds.

It would have been reassuring.

She found it even less reassuring when there wasn't anyone waiting for her.

Well, so, Alex was late. He'd gotten held up. An emergency at work, maybe. Or maybe she'd misunderstood where they were supposed to meet. There was a short ferry ride from the airport on Garvina Island across the Tongass Narrows to Ketchikan. He was probably waiting for her there.

She wouldn't think for a minute she was being left practically at the altar for the third time, with time running out.

"You're going to chew a hole in your lip." A warm voice she was beginning to find familiar offered the warning from behind her.

Cass whirled to face the source of that voice. She lifted her chin a notch higher and did her best to look cool and aloof. Considering how little practice she had at it, she thought she pulled the look off fairly well.

"Stood up by lover boy?" The unrepentant and undiscouraged charmer continued with an expression of mock shock in his glinting eyes. "What kind of a man would stand up a woman like you?"

All of them, Cass felt like sobbing out.

She settled for glaring at Jason and looking for her dog. At least she still had Rex, she consoled herself. *He* was loyal. *He* loved her.

He was also woozy. Freed, he let out a mournful howl and dragged all four feet, claws scratching in protest, while three male airline attendants winced and hauled him along.

Even woozy, Rex put up quite a fight.

The sight made her smile. "Here, puppy," she crooned.

The sound had an electrifying effect on the huge mutt. He abruptly stopped fighting and, before the men could recover, lunged frantically in the direction of the beloved, familiar voice.

Jason thought the huge, slavering wolf-like beast was going to disembowel his newfound fiancée before anyone could stop it.

It leaped on her and he fully expected to see her toppled and mauled. Making a move to intercept the beast, he failed to stop the dog and merely succeeded in toppling her to the floor himself. They went down in a tangle of man, woman and dog, and the dog, if it was actually a dog, let out an even worse howl before doing violence to the leg of Jason's jeans.

His one coherent thought was, thank God for the sturdy threads of Levi Strauss.

"Down!" Cass roared out. "Down, boy!"

Jason gave her a look of patent disbelief. "Down? I'm risking my life, not to mention my leg to save you from that— that—" he broke off and demanded incredulously, "What the hell is that thing?"

She closed her eyes, knit her brows and said in the exhausted-of-patience tone of voice mainly reserved for incorrigible children, "Not you. Rex." Then she yelled again, "Down!"

With a pitiful whine, the beast turned bloodshot eyes at her in a canine plea.

"No." Her voice was level and firm.

It whined again. But it dropped its gaping jaw and released Jason's jeans.

"Rex? You named it Rex?" Jason stared at her. "That's your dog? You call that thing a dog?"

She gave him a look he was beginning to recognize already. "He's not a thing. He's a dog. And yes, he's mine."

Jason believed it when the thing literally groveled on its hairy belly and whined again.

"Bad puppy," Cass told it.

It managed to sink even lower, all the while fixing pleading eyes on her and wagging the ragged tail.

"I'm sorry he chewed on your pants," she informed Jason. "But he thought you were attacking me. He wouldn't have bitten you. He was just trying to hold you."

"He thought *I* was attacking you?" Was he hearing this right?

"Well, you jumped on me and knocked me over," Cass pointed out.

"Listen, *he* jumped on you and knocked you over. *I* was trying to keep you from being lunch!"

"Oh, never mind. Just get off me."

Jason moved to comply. He liked the position they were in, but next time he got her horizontal it'd be minus the hard floor and the dog and he'd have her full attention.

The canine was watching him and it looked hungry. He wasn't about to give it an excuse to sink those yellow teeth into something more substantial than a pair of jeans.

Without stopping to consider that he was risking life and limb, Jason extended a hand to pull her to her feet as soon as he'd regained his. It was a reflex. Maybe he hadn't had a mother for long, but she'd taught him manners. And something about this woman made him want to play the chivalrous rescuer and protector. Once she was standing, he found himself not wanting to release her hand. Wanting to keep it in his.

Such a small thing. It was just her hand. And her man-eating beast was watching and waiting to pounce.

Still, he prolonged the moment, savoring the warmth and

sweetness of her slender hand resting in his square one. He found he liked her hand as well as he liked the rest of her. Soft, yet capable. Durable and sturdy and still somehow fragile and precious. She was all soft feminine warmth, but not the insubstantial kind. Hers wasn't the softness of weakness, but the gentleness that came only from a deep source of strength.

He wanted to hold on to her and never let go.

He wanted to kiss her. Gently. Carefully. A wooing kiss to coax her lips into softening for his. A tender kiss. A kiss of feeling. A kiss of discovery. He wanted to cherish her with worshipful kisses from head to toe.

And then he wanted to ravish and devour her and fuck her mindless.

The realization startled him into practically tossing her hand away as if burned.

She gave him an offended look, placed her hand far from his reach, straightened herself and then turned her attention to the dog.

At one soft word, it leaped to its feet and went to her, but this time a little less over-enthusiastically.

Jason thought for a moment that he could relate to the dog's feeling. His canine world revolved around her, and the obedience was obviously born of love and earnest willingness to please.

When Cass rewarded him with petting and praise, Jason felt ridiculously jealous of the animal.

Was this what he was going to be reduced to for the rest of his life? Sitting up and begging for her attention? Competing with the world's most hideous dog?

The dog was absolutely not sleeping in their bed. Jason made up his mind firmly that instant. Not in the bed. Not in the bedroom. No, no, a thousand times no. He'd be damned if he'd share her in there. The dog could sleep outside.

Well, maybe not outside. But outside the bedroom door. He'd be very clear with his wife about that.

As soon as he made her his wife. It couldn't be soon enough for Jason's peace of mind. With every second that passed, the risk of exposure went up. He couldn't let her find out the truth until after he had a ring safely on her finger, the vows said and the proper papers signed.

And the marriage sealed. Improperly.

At the thought of kissing her and claiming her publicly and legally and then privately in ways possibly illegal in certain southern states, he nearly lost the ability to think, let alone plan. He shoved those thoughts aside and focused all his attention on the problem at hand.

He had to get her up in front of the proper authority. Fast. And with a plausible excuse. Where the hell was Sam?

As if in answer to his thoughts, the man appeared and relief thundered through him. Everything would work out just fine. They'd come up with a plan and they'd convince her to go through with the wedding before she could ask any dangerous questions and then...

Well, then he'd think of what to do next.

But it was going to involve kissing.

Full-body contact, roll-on-the-floor kissing.

Hot, sweet, wild, wet kissing that made their hearts pound and their heads weak so that they'd have to break apart to take a deep breath and re-oxygenate their bloodstreams before starting all over again.

Dizzy, aching, wanting, breathless and greedy kissing.

It was only reasonable. That way, her lips would be fully

occupied, so she could hardly scream *Liar!* at him. Also, she'd be too dazed to sic her dog on him or walk out.

Now that the dog was calmed and reassured, she turned to thank the men for bringing him out and apologize for the trouble he'd caused, and Jason was struck again by the unbelievable depth of his luck.

She was a true lady.

A lady thought about other people.

A lady was gracious.

His lady had class in spades. He didn't deserve her, but he wasn't about to let her get away, since Fate had seen fit to bring her to him.

What was he supposed to do, step aside for Mountain Man Mason? No. Never. He was the one who'd lured her to Alaska and she was his by all rights. His emails had persuaded her, not the photograph. In fact, she might just have been so enamored of his emails she was actually willing to overlook the photograph. Yes, that was it, Jason decided.

Besides, Mountain Man Mason didn't have a genuine classic frontier bordello and saloon to offer her. He had a log cabin and a look-out tower by way of the US Forestry Service. No domestic challenge at all. He didn't think Mason had an inch of grout anywhere.

She'd gone to so much trouble to learn about grout, she certainly deserved some of her own to work on.

"Sam," he murmured with a nod as the other man drew even with him.

"Jase," Sam replied, "What in the world is that creature and have the proper authorities been notified?"

Jason expelled a long breath. "That, my friend, is her dog."

Sam stared, shocked. "Her dog?"

"Her dog." Then Jason directed his full attention to the other man. "If you're here, who's tending bar?"

"Nobody. The Last Resort is closed due to a wedding."

"A wedding is just the time when someone might need a bit of bolstering," Jason pointed out.

Sam nodded sagely. "I know. I brought you a seltzer." He handed Jason a paper cup with a plastic lid and a straw.

"Ah."

"We've got a cake, but it isn't exactly a wedding cake," Sam went on. "We sort of had to make do with what we had. The baker swore at me in seven languages when I asked for a wedding cake in one hour, so I asked for whatever was available."

"And what was available?" Jason asked, his eyes still following his intended.

Sam coughed. "Ah, well, it seems there was a party canceled. A bachelor party. Canceled due to the fiancée finding out about it."

"Hm."

Sam shot the other man a quick glance and noted with some relief that he was too caught up in watching his little woman to ask any more questions. He did hope Jason would appreciate that he'd convinced Mona Jeffries not to jump out of the cake in question as planned.

It hadn't been easy, either. Mona didn't get many opportunities to be the star attraction these days, now that Creek Street had turned respectable. She settled for being the town scarlet woman, but it just didn't have the same distinction it had once offered.

Everyone in town knew Mona and knew she was a frustrated actress, an artist and an advocate of free expression.

A performance artist, she'd called herself when she moved there from New York.

Sam believed in calling a stripper a stripper, but Mona's feelings would be hurt. She was proud of her former occupation. It had nearly broken her heart when she'd had to quit to pacify her ex-husband and the judge presiding over their custody battle. She contented herself with raising her son and raising Cain at the local PTA meetings, but they all knew she still longed for the bright lights she'd left behind.

So of course she'd been thrilled to be offered a job jumping out of a cake at a bachelor party.

And of course, she'd shared her excitement.

So, of course, Patty Weston, the fiancée, had heard about the bachelor party and Mona's part in it, and threatened to call off the wedding if the party wasn't called off.

Mona was terribly disappointed.

So were the members of the planned party in question.

Still, it meant they had a wedding cake, of sorts, on short notice. He'd been assured it was edible, and that was what mattered.

They also had the Reverend Moonbeam to perform the ceremony. True, he was a reverend of the Rainbow Church, but he was still legally empowered by the State of Alaska to join together two consenting adults in holy matrimony.

Sam didn't think Jason would object. He didn't have any strong affiliation to any particular church. Or if he did, he hadn't said so.

Overall, Sam thought he'd done a splendid job of organizing the wedding. The Lawrences had helped. So had most of Jason's neighbors and clientele. Even Mona had pitched in— she'd donated the bridal lingerie for the wedding night along with a gift bag full of what she called "essentials" from a shop she assured Sam catered to these occasions.

Sam had taken a look in the bag and wondered if maybe they'd gone a little overboard preparing The Last Resort for the happy occasion, but then again, it *was* a former bordello.

Mona had proclaimed it all terribly romantic.

And Sam hadn't had the heart to make a scathing, cynical retort.

The truth was, romance seemed to have found its way into the whole town. He'd put it down to spring fever, but it was closer to summer.

A midsummer night's dream, perhaps, the English teacher reflected. An unfamiliar sense of something that might have been nostalgia stirred deep within.

But it certainly wasn't romance. He wasn't about to fall victim to that idea ever again. Miss Lonely Hearts had been his one and only lapse, and it wouldn't be repeated.

Still, it did seem as if something good was going to come out of his misadventure, and for Jason's sake, he was glad.

Marriage might not be for him, but it was certainly in the cards for Jason. Marriage suited him. He was a settled-down, made-for-matrimony man if there ever was one.

Jason didn't smoke, drink or chase women. He minded his business and kept up The Last Resort as a local institution, just the way it should be.

He was also lonely. And very taken with one lovely blonde.

He needed a wife. She needed a husband. It was so perfect, Sam could very nearly empathize with Mona.

He disregarded the minor complications involved. True love hadn't gone smoothly for Romeo. Why should it be any easier for one bartender?

And if the worst occurred, why, a bit of tragedy might win some of the adults over to his Thursday evening literature class.

But for Jason's sake, he hoped for the best.

The way he couldn't take his eyes off of the blonde, that seemed likely.

The blonde evidently noticed the staring, and she came up to Jason with the incredible beast at her heels.

"Why are you watching me?"

Jason looked innocent. "Watching you? I was looking out the window."

Her dark blue eyes narrowed. "You were watching me."

"All right, I was watching you. You make a better view than anything outside the window."

Sam nodded in agreement. "When you can't see Deer Mountain—"

Jason abruptly cut him off by simultaneously jabbing him in the ribs and stomping on one foot.

Sam gave him a hurt look.

Cass gave him The Look. The Look every man wants to avoid. "That was incredibly rude," she informed Jason. "Let the poor man speak."

"I'll let him speak when he has something to say," Jason muttered. "Do you have something to say, Sam?"

"I do. I regret to inform the lady that her fiancé has been unavoidably detained," Sam orated.

Jason warned him with a glance not to overdo it.

Cass didn't notice. Vulnerable confusion shone in her sweet face, and her voice wobbled when she prompted, "Detained?"

Sam stepped forward to take her arm in a reassuring hold, then cast a glance at the dog and thought better of it. "Not to worry, dear lady. He wanted to reassure you of his honorable intentions and so he asked that you marry him immediately by proxy."

He turned to Jason, as if the idea had only now occurred to him. "You can stand in for Alex, can't you?"

Jason fixed his warm gaze on Cass. "It would be my pleasure."

She nibbled at her lower lip again. "I don't know." Then, "How did you know who I was?"

"Your fiancé sent me. He showed me your picture so I'd know who to look for," Sam said. "And if I may say so, it doesn't do you justice. Come, my dear, if you have any doubts about your future husband's good character, the entire town will be glad to serve as character references. He's a good man. I know him very well myself."

Mingled doubt and hope were reflected in her eyes. "You do?"

"I do. I can personally assure you he means to honor the commitment he's asked you to make and your agreement will make him the happiest of men."

Jason frowned at him. As if the man thought he was laying it on a little thick.

"Does he have any kind of criminal record?"

"He's a veritable pillar of the community."

Still, she hesitated. "What about any...well, does he have any bad habits?"

Sam cleared his throat. "Ah. That would depend on what you consider bad habits. I don't know from personal experience, but the chances are fairly good that he leaves his socks on the floor and leaves the toilet seat up. He's been a bachelor for some time."

Cass blushed.

Jason thought it was charming. She blushed at the mere mention of such intimate details as socks on the floor and where the seat was left? She hadn't ever lived with another man. That was a dead giveaway.

He couldn't have been more delighted.

"I meant, does he, well..." She trailed off and Sam nodded in understanding.

"He isn't a drinking man. He's never been known to abuse a woman. He isn't the type to run around. He's also solvent and Parker Wyatt, the local bank president, will testify that his credit history is sound."

Jason thought Sam could be a convincing con artist himself. Enough to give Miss Lonely Hearts a run for her money. Or rather, for other people's money. Not that Sam lied, exactly. His reputation was sound enough. And he did, in fact, leave his socks on the floor, but he made a mental note to remember to leave the seat in the proper position always, from that day forward till death did they part.

She knit her brows together in concern. "How is he with children?"

"Well, now. I've never seen him with children," Sam had to admit. "But he's good with people. He always remembers little details and has a way of making everyone feel important."

That surprised Jason. He did? It wasn't much of a trick to remember what each person liked to drink. Regulars liked to know their preferences were noticed. It was just good business. And he enjoyed the friendly atmosphere of his bar, the good-natured gossip, the give-and-take and easy flow of conversation. He'd spent a lifetime noticing and memorizing details and learning to read people. It was second nature by now. Nothing special about that.

But she seemed impressed.

"If he's good with people and makes them feel important, he'll do the same with children," she decided.

"I'm confident he'll be as successful at parenthood as he is at everything else he's set his mind on," Sam concurred.

She nodded slowly. "All right. I'll marry him by proxy."

Jason couldn't resist teasing her. "Wouldn't you rather marry me?"

He wasn't prepared for the total rejection in her decided "No".

Ridiculously, it hurt.

"Why not?"

"Because."

The uninformative response was hardly satisfying "Because? What kind of reason is that?"

She gave him a steady look. "Because I've made a commitment and I intend to honor it, for starters. How do you think Alex would feel if he came back and found me married to you instead?"

"That's the chance he took when he left you in the lurch," Jason shot back.

"He did not leave me in the lurch." Storm clouds gathered in her eyes. "He was unavoidably detained. And he made other arrangements. He sent someone to meet me and explain."

"How do you know he isn't hiding something?" Jason inquired. "Suspicious, isn't it? A man doesn't show up for his own wedding?"

He regretted it when her lower lip trembled. Her chin lifted proudly higher. "It couldn't be helped," she managed to say.

He cursed inwardly. Not tears. He hadn't meant to reduce

her to practically weeping over being left unmet by her intended at the airport and stuck with a stand-in at her own wedding. He looked at her quivering lip and softened.

"No, it couldn't be helped," he agreed. He turned to Sam with an air of expectation. "When and where is this ceremony taking place?"

"The high school gymnasium. In one hour. Reception following. And it's time to catch the ferry now. Right this way, please." Sam officiously ushered them both on their way, with the slavering monster dogging their heels. "Ms. Mona has kindly offered the bride the use of her house to get ready. I'll drop you off," he said directly to Cass.

She nodded.

"And Jason, I'll take you home to get ready yourself. Then I'll drive you, and Mona will bring the bride."

"What about the dog?" Jason wanted to know.

Sam turned to Cass. "Will he stay put if you tell him to?"

She nodded again. She seemed a little nervous. A little jittery. Suddenly, Jason didn't like the idea of letting her out of his sight.

She might be having second thoughts.

She might not show up at the school.

Sam seemed to notice, and patted her hand. "Nervous? Ah. Well, what bride wouldn't be? But I promise you, you won't regret it. You'll be in good hands."

Yes, Jason agreed. She'd be in good hands. The best hands.

She'd be in his.

With an effort, he resisted the urge to rub them together in diabolical glee.

She'd be in his hands, and if she just gave them a chance, she might decide she liked being there. Might? She would. Of course she would. There was enough electricity between them to power the whole island

But Jason wished somebody would notice that he was feeling a little nervous and jittery himself.

Chapter Six

An hour later, a very confused Cass found herself walking up the temporary aisle formed by folding chairs towards her far-too-hard-to-ignore former seatmate.

He still looked too attractive. Too virile. Too...male.

She didn't want to notice another man at her own wedding. What kind of a wife would that make her? Was she falling into the same unforgivable, traitorous habits shared by Tom and Matthew? Was she so warped from her experiences that she'd become incapable of fidelity herself? And how had she ended up here, when she'd planned to meet the man in person first, before things went any further?

Ever since she'd gotten on the plane, it was as if she'd taken some irrevocable step into a stream of events and the current had yanked her along, rushing forward before she could catch her balance or even think.

She could pinpoint the exact moment when she'd lost control of the situation. That would be when she found herself laying under Jason and really enjoying it. So much she'd almost done something crazy. With him. In public. Instead, she'd leaped at Sam's explanations and plans and now here she was. Walking down the aisle. Which, come to think of it, still qualified as doing something crazy with Jason in public.

He took her arm when she reached him, and that was even

worse. An electric sensation of awareness spread from that innocent point of contact until she could have sworn every nerve in her body was charged and attuned to his presence.

Chemistry, she told herself. *It's nothing but chemistry. And you're susceptible because you're a little nervous and a little unsure just now and you've had no sex or dull sex for the last year which you obviously should have done something about or you wouldn't be reacting this way.*

She was definitely nervous.

The man who'd introduced himself as Sam Weiss, a local teacher, had whisked her away, deftly seen to her luggage and her dog and offered smooth explanations all at the same time. Then he'd delivered her into the care of a woman named Mona who could give Demi Moore a run for the title of sexiest mother.

The woman intimidated her.

The whole situation unsettled her.

She wished Alex was there to reassure her that she wasn't making a horrible mistake.

Reverend Moonshine, or whatever his name was, didn't do anything to relieve her anxiety. The man wore a toga and love beads. His head was entirely bald, and he wore a full and flowing snow-white beard that made him vaguely resemble an Old Testament prophet.

Cass had the sneaking suspicion he'd been partaking of his namesake, too. That, or his dreamy expression was due to something even more degenerate than some local home-brew.

It would have given the whole scenario a sense of normalcy if she'd been in a traditional wedding dress and if her stand-in groom had dressed equally formally.

Or maybe the traditional trappings would only have made the rest of the setting stand out even more bizarrely in contrast.

Instead of a quiet church filled with flowers, they were in an echoing gymnasium filled with the unmistakable scent of sweat socks.

The groom wasn't even present.

The reverend was likely to go into a trance or pass out in the middle of the service.

And she was wearing blue jeans, for the something blue, a far from conservative white eyelet midriff blouse from Mona for the something borrowed, new white lace briefs for the something new, and a battered pair of sneakers for the something old. A bouquet of dried flowers and decorative comb with silk flowers, faux pearls and white bridal netting completed the outfit.

Her stand-in wore a new pair of jeans in place of the pair Rex had desecrated. He'd exchanged the sweater for a form-fitting green knit polo shirt, casually open at the throat.

He was tanned and taut and far, far too attractive.

On second thought, Cass was glad he wasn't in formal dress. It might have been just too overwhelming.

As if sensing her slowly building panic, he gave her a solemn wink and murmured for her ears alone, "Don't worry. This won't hurt a bit, and it'll all be over in a minute. Be brave."

She gave him a withering look.

He smiled and the golden flecks in his eyes danced.

The reverend cleared his throat, closed his eyes, raised his hands and began the intonation.

"Dearly beloved, we are gathered here today to witness the joining together of..." he paused, and blinked in some confusion.

"Cassandra Adams," Jason prompted.

"Thank you. Of Cassandra Adams and..." he trailed off

again.

"Alexander," Jason supplied

"And Alexander."

"Alex Sanders," Cass corrected.

The reverend looked faintly surprised. "That's what I said." Then, more loudly, "To join these two in holy matrimony."

"Not *us* two," Cass objected, feeling panicky again. "I'm not marrying him."

"Yes, you are," the reverend assured her.

"No, I'm not! I'm marrying Alex Sanders."

"Certainly," the gentle man agreed. He exchanged an ageless look with Jason, who gave a slight shrug in reply and mouthed "Nerves," while Cass was distracted.

"To join these two in holy matrimony," Reverend Moonbeam repeated. "If any here object, let him or her speak now or forever hold his or her peace."

"I object," Cass broke in, a tinge of desperation in her voice.

"You can't object. You're the bride," Reverend Moonbeam explained patiently. "The question is for any other person present who objects."

"But—"

"Wait until it's your turn," he told her in a firm voice.

She subsided unhappily.

No other objections were forthcoming, so the ceremony proceeded. All too soon, Jason nudged her and she nearly jumped out of her skin and dropped her bouquet. "What?" she demanded, glaring at him and waiting for an explanation.

"It's your turn now," the reverend replied instead. "You speak."

"I do?" Cass stared at him, amazed. It was her turn

already?

"She does, and I witness it," Revered Moonbeam told Jason. "Give her the ring."

"But—"

Her protestation was cut off and overridden as the man's voice rose and drowned her out. "As you place it on her finger, you say, 'With this ring, I thee wed'."

Jason hastily complied. "With this ring, I thee wed."

Then he pressed another cold piece of metal into her hand and Cass opened her hand to stare at it blindly. "What—" she began, but again she was interrupted.

"You put it on him and repeat after me," the reverend informed her. "With this ring, I thee wed."

"But—"

"Just say it," Jason hissed.

Fumbling, she managed to grasp the plain gold circle and place it on the blunt, square hand offered to her. "With this ring, I thee wed," she mumbled.

Reverend Moonbeam heaved a sigh of relief and hastily got out, "By-the-power-vested-in-me-I-now-pronounce-you-man-and-wife-what-the-Diety-of-your-choice-has-joined-together-let-no-man-tear-apart-you-may-kiss-the-bride."

Cass stared at him, then Jason in shock.

Just like that? It was over? She was married? Who was she married to, Alex or this man?

"See? It's all over, and it didn't hurt at all," the stranger at her side murmured.

Then he kissed her.

Cass thought that was going too far, even if he was standing in. Even if it was traditional for the male guests to claim a kiss from the bride.

He cupped her chin in one of his warm, square hands, slid the other against the small of her back, bare thanks to Mona, and the touch was disturbingly erotic and intimate. He lowered his warm, firm lips to hers and moved them gently over her mouth. The kiss set off a series of tingling shocks that leaped from her lips to her nipples and then went south. Her sex reacted with a pulse of heat and when he released her mouth, she put one hand to her lips, wide-eyed.

"You shouldn't have done that," she whispered.

"I should have done that hours ago," he answered, unrepentant. "Do I get to carry you over the threshold now?"

She glared at him. "You don't get to carry me anywhere."

"Really? I'm sure I remember something about carrying off the bride in wedding traditions," Jason mused.

Reverend Moonbeam nodded in agreement. "The tradition of carrying the bride over the threshold is a symbolic remembrance of the rape of the Sabine women in Roman times."

Cass gasped.

The reverend hastened to reassure her. "Rape merely means the forcible taking of, not violent assault, although it has come to have a more specific meaning in these times. The Romans needed wives, and Roman women were in short supply." He gave Jason a mild frown. "We of the Rainbow Church do not condone violence in any form."

"I'm a pacifist myself," he replied cheerfully. "I just want to make sure I carry out all the traditions in the proper form. I'm a traditional kind of man."

"Mm, yes. Unfortunately, the tradition of showering the bridal couple with rice to symbolize the blessings of fertility has been discontinued for ecological reasons," the reverend warned. "However, I'd be happy to perform a substitute fertility rite of your choice. No extra charge."

"No, that's all right," Cass rushed out.

"Are you sure?" Jason asked. He looked as hopeful, as pleading as her dog. The rat.

"Positive."

He sighed and turned back to Reverend Moonbeam. "No fertility rite, but thank you for offering."

The man bowed his gleaming pate gracefully. "You're welcome."

"You're disgusting," Cass hissed at him once the reverend was out of earshot.

"I'm only trying to carry out all my obligations as the groom," he protested.

"Yes, well, you're going too far," she snapped.

"You have no sense of humor," her stand-in groom sighed. "Pity. Come on, we have to sign the papers."

"*I* have to sign. *You* don't sign anything," she protested.

"Yes, I do. I'm the proxy. This is a marriage by proxy. You want to be married legally, don't you?"

She hesitated. "Well, yes. I think. I mean, yes. But—"

"Then we have to sign the paperwork and have the witnesses sign. Come on."

So she let him lead her off and press a pen between her numb fingers.

She signed.

He signed, with a flourish.

Sam Weiss signed.

And Mona signed, while sniffling and dabbing at her eyes

with a delicate, lacy white handkerchief.

Then Jason slid an envelope into the reverend's hand with a final nod of thanks, and took Cass's arm to lead her away in the general direction of the long folding table set up against one wall. "You look pale," he informed her. "Do you want some punch?"

She nodded, mute.

The punch was refreshing. She had one cup, then another. Then a third. Strange, but now that the ceremony was over, she was feeling much more positive about the whole thing. In fact, the event seemed to have taken on a kind of warm, golden glow.

When Jason swept her onto the floor for a dance, she didn't protest.

Well, she was tired, she defended herself silently. It helped to have someone to support her. His strong, lean frame did that very well as he guided her in time to the music. Gradually, however, she became all too aware of the way his thighs brushed hers, the way her breasts brushed against his chest. The warmth of his hand placed firmly against the bare hollow of her lower back. Her breasts felt swollen and aching with the need to be touched. An ache that was echoed low in her pelvis. She wanted to tilt her hips to press against him and do something to relieve that ache.

And then she felt anything but relaxed.

"You're tense," he murmured, his warm breath fanning her cheek and making her shiver. "Put your head on my shoulder."

"No."

"Come on," he coaxed. "What could happen? We're in a room full of people."

"We're in a room full of people who know my husband and are wondering what kind of a woman he's married." Cass pulled back and gave him a discouraging frown. "You're going to have everyone gossiping about my marriage. About my husband."

His brows arced up. "You're concerned about your husband's reputation? The same man who isn't even here?"

"Of course I'm concerned about his reputation. I took his name. I have to respect it, and so do you. And he'd be here if he could."

She broke off the dance altogether and stood with her arms folded, lecturing him.

"I certainly hope you aren't a friend of Alex's. What kind of man would make a pass at another man's bride during her wedding reception?"

She was wonderful, Jason thought, dazed. She was defending him. Well, she thought she was defending someone else, but it was the thought that counted.

Now he just had to get her eased into the idea of seeing him as the man she was so fiercely defending.

Unfortunately, he had absolutely no idea how to tell her she was really married to him and he'd really never intended to get married. Well, at least not until he'd met her, he corrected mentally. Then the idea had seemed not just attractive but downright predetermined.

However he put it, though, the news was bound to upset her.

He hated to think about just how upset she'd be.

Now she was frowning. "I'm thirsty."

Jason caught her arm as she headed towards the punch bowl and led her towards a water fountain instead. "I don't think you want any more punch."

"Yes, I do."

"It's spiked."

"Spiked?" She swung back to face him, startled. She blinked in obvious confusion.

Jason nodded. "Spiked. You, sweetheart, are on your way to tipsy. Why don't you drink some water?"

She was still staring at him. "Spiked?" She repeated the question as if the word was unknown to her, and utterly confusing.

He couldn't suppress a grin. "Yep. And in my capacity as official proxy husband, I feel it's only right to keep you from dancing on the tables. In public, at least. What you do in private is up to your own judgment. I have a lampshade that would look stunning on you if you get the urge to run wild later."

"Husband?" She gave herself a slight shake and frowned at him again. "You aren't my husband. You aren't. I didn't marry you. I married Alex." She pronounced each word deliberately and carefully so that he couldn't mistake her meaning.

"That isn't the subject," he informed her.

"It isn't?"

"No. You're thirsty. You wanted some water." He tugged on her arm to indicate the way to the water fountain. She followed after a brief hesitation.

He held the button down for her to produce a steady stream, and thought again that this woman brought out his chivalrous instincts. Masculine instincts. That was it, he decided, watching her drink. She made him feel strong. Male. Protective. Capable and caring. He wanted to care for her and cherish her. She was his woman, and she made him aware of his own masculinity on a level he hadn't experienced before.

She was his wife.

He was her husband.

When she straightened, he brushed at the drops of moisture clinging to the corner of her mouth and thought, *today I am a man.* A dead man, once she found out about the lying. But still, a man.

It was a rite of passage. Always before this day, he'd been free of care and unburdened by responsibility for anybody other than himself.

Now everything had changed. He wasn't a single man anymore. He was a husband, the head of a fledgling family.

It felt good. More than that, it felt right.

He could only hope that she'd share his point of view. Eventually. On the positive side, all signs indicated that the sex between them was going to be spectacular and if that didn't help convince her it could at least probably distract her and keep her from dwelling on any possible downside to their arrangement until she got used to the idea.

"Why did you want to marry Alex?" he found himself asking.

A kaleidoscope of expressions raced across her face. She bit her lip and turned away. "Because."

"That's what you said when I asked you why you wouldn't marry me," Jason pointed out. "It isn't much of an answer."

She frowned at him.

He tugged her back towards the dance floor, thinking it might be easier to get her talking if he kept her distracted. She went along with him, moving lightly to the music and following his lead with unconscious grace, as if they'd been dancing together for years.

Finally, she said, "Why do you keep asking me questions like that?"

He did his best to look innocent. "I'm a bartender. It's

customary for anyone and everyone to confide in me. It goes with the territory. People tell me their troubles. I listen. It has the same sacred seal of silence as a confessional or a therapist's couch without the price tag or the possibility of penance." He smiled at her and added, "Besides, it might do you good to talk about it. I can tell you're worried. You keep chewing on your lip."

She halted, startled, and swung wide eyes to meet his. "I do?"

"You do. If I were playing poker with you, I'd win every hand. You'd never be able to get away with a bluff."

Cass responded to the subtle guiding pressure of his hand on her waist and resumed dancing. Still, she didn't say anything.

"Okay," Jason said, serious, "I apologize for teasing you. You just looked so nervous, I thought it would help if I could make you laugh."

She glanced up again, questioning.

"On the plane," he expounded.

"Oh." She nodded. "It's okay. I was nervous. I *am* nervous. I'm sorry, too."

He smiled. "Can we start over? Hello. I'm Jason."

Cass smiled back. A small smile, but he thought it was a start.

"Hello. I'm Cassandra."

"Nice name."

"Thank you."

"Kind of an unlucky one, though. Why'd your parents choose that name?" Jason wondered out loud.

She shrugged. "I guess they thought the chances of me turning into a mad prophetess were pretty slim."

He threw his head back and laughed.

"Also, I think they were pretty sure no Olympian deities would show up in Port Townsend, Washington. The town doesn't have that kind of history. Environmental activists, yes. Vengeful gods, no."

She said it so deadpan, it nearly killed him. And he'd accused her of lacking a sense of humor.

"They were right, too," she continued. "I have absolutely no talent for soothsaying. I don't see the future coming until it hits me in the face." She sighed and tucked her head against his shoulder.

Jason almost stopped dead, but recovered himself and did his best to seem casual. As if there was nothing unusual about it. As if he didn't consider the small, trusting gesture the single most precious gift he'd ever received.

"That sounds like the beginning of a story," he prodded.

Cass nodded, her hair brushing his chin as she did. Along with a bit of white netting. He smoothed it back and commented, "Nice touch, the comb. Did Mona do your hair?"

"Yes. She said it went with an outfit she had." She raised her head to meet his eyes. "What kind of an outfit would she wear a bridal headpiece with?"

Jason's lips twitched, but he kept his expression solemn. "I'm not sure you really want to know. Tell you what, you tell me your story, and I'll tell you about Mona."

"Was I telling you my story?"

"Yes. You were about to tell me why you wanted to marry Alex. And don't say *because*. You've already said that twice."

"Sorry. Am I repeating myself?"

"You're stalling. Spill it, or I'll start telling the story for you," he warned.

"You would," Cass muttered. "You and your verbal potshots. 'Alaska's an extension of the old west'," she mimicked with sharp sarcasm. "Well, you were right. I'm moving away from bad memories and bad decisions. Although that's not the whole story. I'm also moving to new opportunities. Are you happy now?"

Jason tightened his hold on her unconsciously, then realized what he was doing and carefully relaxed. Her words stirred up too many altogether alarming possibilities. What kind of bad decisions? What kind of bad memories? Were any of them likely to follow her?

"Go on."

"Go on? You aren't satisfied with that?" She raised her head to glare at him. Then she shrugged. "Maybe you are a friend of Alex's."

She was silent for another long minute. Then she said, "I'm going to be a good wife. If you're worried about that, you can stop."

He wasn't, actually. Well, not about what kind of a wife she'd make, just about keeping her *his* wife. Now, there was a worry.

Cass went on with quiet determination, "I'm going to make him a very happy man."

Jason was unspeakably happy to hear it.

"And I am not on the rebound. I have no feelings whatsoever for any other man in my past."

The fiercely determined words turned him cold.

Man in her past. Men in her past? Bad decisions, she'd said.

What else had she said?

That she didn't see the future coming until it hit her in the face.

That what she wanted and valued most in a husband was honesty.

"You were supposed to marry somebody else. And he cheated on you," Jason stated softly as the inescapable conclusion dawned.

She stared at him for a minute in mingled hurt and surprise.

Then her eyes filled with tears.

Chapter Seven

He'd made her cry.

Jason wanted to groan out loud. If he wanted to make a good impression as a husband, so far he wasn't doing very well.

His bride was very quietly and politely sobbing on his shoulder.

He supposed it had been a mistake to remind her of something that was obviously a deep source of personal humiliation. And hurt.

"I'm sorry," she said into his shoulder, struggling for control. "You don't even know me. This is so embarrassing."

He tucked her head closer to his chest and tightened his arms imperceptibly around her, shielding her. To anyone who cared to look, they looked like any other dancing couple. "Don't be sorry. Go ahead, cry. Get it all out. It might do you good."

Cass made a faint half-laughing, half-choking sound. "First you tell me it'll do me good to talk to you. Then you tell me it would do me good to cry on you. Next you'll tell me that it would do me good to let you console me some other way."

He smiled, despite himself. "I admit the idea has some appeal. I can't believe any man in his right mind would refuse an opportunity to console you in any way you'd agree to. But you have a very low opinion of men in general if you think it isn't possible for one to make an honest offer of friendship."

There he went, lying again. Jason resigned himself to doing a lot more of it, too. But it wasn't completely untrue. Yes, he had designs on her, but not the way she implied. And he was trying to be a friend. In his opinion, husbands and wives ought to be best friends. Besides, she obviously needed a friend.

She hesitated briefly. Then she relaxed against him, and the difference made his head spin.

He'd had her in his arms all along. But with an attitude of polite formality. A bit stiff, even. Wanting to be sure he didn't get the wrong idea or try to take advantage.

Now she relaxed, coming full against him. Her body rested against his without resistance. Her arms held his waist, lightly. Holding, not tensed and ready to push away. He could feel the soft weight of her breasts against his chest, the gentle curve of her hips tucked close to his, the length of her legs brushing his as they moved.

Cass, soft and trusting.

She took his breath away.

She nearly broke his heart. Especially when she spoke again.

"I'm sorry. You're right. I promised myself I wouldn't let anything turn me bitter and cynical. You're being very kind to me, and I appreciate it."

Then she lifted her face and smiled at him, and she did break his heart.

Right down the center.

Jason thought he could hear it crack and separate as she went on, "I'd like us to be friends."

She was so sweet, her eyes luminous with tears, her face raised to his, her full lower lip curved in a rueful half smile.

110

He wanted to kiss her until she lost her breath.

Somehow, he resisted.

But he couldn't resist raising a hand to her cheek. He slid his thumb below a tear-bright eye, moisture darkening her lashes, and gently wiped away the tears. First one side, then the other. Then he held her face in both hands and just smiled at her.

"You shouldn't cry today," Jason told her.

She wrinkled her nose. "You said I should. Get it all out."

"And I meant it, then. I brought up a painful subject. Telling you to bottle it up would just make it worse. However, you're feeling better now and brides should wear smiles, not tears."

She was feeling better, Cass decided.

"Speaking of what brides should wear, explain about Mona and the mysterious bridal headpiece," she suggested. Then she settled her cheek back against his now-damp shoulder, feeling more relaxed and peaceful than she had in weeks, since her former fiancé had simultaneously dumped her and plunged her into unemployment and chaos. From that point on, nothing in her life had been the same and there hadn't been time to catch her balance.

"I don't know," Jason mused. "I'm pretty sure there's more to your story. We had a deal, didn't we?"

She laughed. "You'd make a really good reporter, do you know that? You just keep digging." She looked at him again, teasing, "Friends don't harp on sensitive subjects. In fact, really good friends often provide convenient distractions at awkward moments."

His eyes gleamed. "And this is a test of my friendship? All right, I'll let you off the hook for now. But just remember that really, really good friends tell everything." He gave her a significant look.

She poked him in the chest. "So start telling. You've made me curious."

He caught her hand and gave her a shaming look. "Watch it, you're resorting to violence. Reverend Moonbeam might catch you at it and be upset. Then what would you do if you decided you needed him to perform a fertility rite over you someday?"

Cass gave him a sweet look. "I'm sure if such a situation ever came up, I could explain to him that sometimes there are extenuating circumstances. I'm sure he'd understand."

"All right. Behave yourself, and I'll tell you. But don't blame me if you don't like it."

"Why wouldn't I like it?" she asked.

"Maybe because Mona used to be a stripper and her most popular costume consisted of a white satin G-string, a waist-length strand of pearls and a modest headpiece of white bridal netting," Jason suggested.

She halted and gave him a narrow look. "You're making that up. I am not wearing part of a stripper's costume at my wedding."

"Oh, yes, you are," he assured her with wicked delight. "And if we get to be really, really, *really* good friends, maybe you'll model the rest of it for me someday?"

His all-too-easy-to-read expression told Cass he was loving her predictable reaction to being told the truth about Mona and the bridal comb.

"I understand the shoes that go with the get-up are really something," he added meaningfully. "White satin pumps with high, high heels. Would you wear those, too?"

As a matter of fact, Mona had had a pair of heels like that

and had tried to get her to wear them.

She had also offered some rather startling marital advice

It made sense now.

"Mona's a stripper?"

Jason chuckled. "She prefers the term performance artist. Or exotic dancer."

"A stripper?" Cass repeated, shocked and at the same time wanting to laugh.

It was so wonderfully ridiculous, the whole situation.

So much so that she did laugh. Full-throated, breathless laughter that brought tears to her eyes and left her leaning weakly against her proxy husband.

And then Sam rolled the cake out, Jason realized simultaneously what it was designed for and that Mona was conspicuously absent and the music changed in a bizarre montage that spelled approaching doom.

He knew what was going to happen.

He was powerless to stop it.

And as the inevitable unfolded, he swore on his mother's memory that if by some miracle his wife didn't get right straight back on the first plane off Revillagigedo and leave him forever, he would move heaven and earth to see to it that she had a real wedding and a real party and a real honeymoon with any and all romantic trappings her heart desired.

It was the least he could do to try to make it up to her that she'd had a stripper jump out of her wedding cake.

"Please. Drink this," Jason was urging.

Cass thought he sounded worried.

She thought he might have reason to be. She'd nearly

fainted. She was just not used to the kinds of shocks she'd had in the last hour, she decided. Not to mention the last day. The last weeks. All the way back to the shock of her broken engagement and right on top of it, the shock of getting fired.

"I've never been fired before," she told Jason, ignoring the punch he was pushing on her. For some reason, that fact seemed very important. She wanted him to believe her.

"Of course not," he agreed. Giving up on the cup of punch, he took her hands and started chafing them. "Maybe you should put your head back down."

Maybe she should. She did. It seemed to help, too. The ring of blackness around her peripheral vision started to fade and she could see green grass and wildflowers.

They were outside, sitting on the field that served for football, baseball and track. Jason had taken one look at her white face and whisked her out for air.

She wondered what it meant that he'd been watching her face instead of Mona's eye-popping performance.

"Never," she repeated, getting back to the subject of her abrupt departure from waitressing. "I've always had high recommendations from everyone I've ever worked for."

Jason made soothing sounds of agreement and continued to restore her circulation.

"Then Tom came into The Atrium during the lunch rush and sat at one of my tables and told me the wedding was off. He was going to marry the boss's daughter instead. Who happens to be my cousin. But he still wanted to sleep with me."

Jason let out a wheezing, choking sound.

Cass didn't notice.

"So I poured a pitcher of ice water over his head and ruined his suit. And then I got fired."

Her voice was calm. Even. Matter-of-fact.

"There aren't a whole lot of openings for a waitress with a bad attitude. All my training is in photography which doesn't qualify me for much in the way of day jobs. I've been dumped twice now. Once right on the day of the wedding." Her calm cracked, and tears started to trickle down her cheeks.

She raised her face to Jason with a watery smile and continued, "I just couldn't go through that again. I didn't want to keep getting it wrong. My personal life wasn't working. It had to change. I had to change. Do something different. So that's why I wanted to marry Alex. At least that way, I thought I'd end up with a decent man and a marriage and a chance at the family I wanted. That sounded better than romantic illusions I didn't see through until everything fell apart on me."

Jason searched through his pockets for a tissue, and finally settled on wiping her cheeks with his hands again.

"That probably sounds really stupid to you," she finished.

"Not really," he said, sliding an arm around her shoulders for a comforting squeeze. "I've heard worse ideas, for less reason."

Cass rested her head on his chest, leaning into the hug. "You aren't just saying that because you're my friend?"

"No." He stroked the silky length of her hair, tangling his fingers in it. Without thinking about it, he pulled her closer, breathing in the light fragrance of sunshine, flowers and woman. His thumb rubbed across her lower lip, testing. Then his mouth replaced it. Tasting.

He could get drunk on kissing her. She went directly to his head. Warm, sweet, so sweet... Jason couldn't resist deepening the kiss, urging her lips to part for him, allowing him to taste the sweet unexplored depths of her mouth. He settled a hand on her waist, smoothing the satin softness of her bare skin in a lingering caress.

Sheer, hungry want rocketed through him. It wasn't enough. It wasn't nearly enough. Urging and urgent, his hands brought her closer, moved over her in restless seeking.

Blood singing, heart pounding, he wanted to lay her down right there in the sun-warmed grass and love her until he'd erased every past unhappiness from her memory, leaving only room for him.

Only for them. The two of them, complete in themselves, a whole world in each other. An unbroken circle.

Cass shivered under the spell of Jason's kiss. She shouldn't be doing this. They shouldn't be doing this. But the way they fit together, the sure way his mouth had found hers, seemed more like the easy familiarity between old lovers than the unsure and tentative exploring of the unknown.

No awkwardness, no false beginnings. He kissed her as if he'd been kissing her for eternity and knew exactly how she liked it best. His square, blunt hands knew just how much pressure to exert to thrill her with the silent message of desire without bruising. Strength tempered by gentleness. Hunger tempered by tenderness.

His mouth roved over hers, drinking in her essence as if she was the nectar of life to him. His hands cradled and stroked as if touching her fulfilled an elemental need.

It was intoxicating after the shattering pain of rejection and betrayal. It would have been easier to give up breathing than to give up the soul-stirring sweetness of this gambler's kiss.

And with wrenching pain, she knew she had to do just that. Because she was committing a betrayal. Making a mockery of the vows she'd barely spoken.

Cass put a hand against his chest and pushed, turning her head away to break the kiss. In response to her silent demand, his hold loosened but he didn't let her go.

"What?"

When she didn't answer right away, Jason brought her back into the circle of his arms and brushed his lips over the crown of her head. She pulled back, but he held fast. "No, Cass, don't."

She gave a wry half laugh. "Don't what?"

"Don't push me away. I'm your friend."

"Friends don't kiss like that."

"If you want me to say I'm sorry, you're going to be disappointed. I'm not sorry. I wanted to kiss you, and you wanted to kiss me. Listen, please." He took her chin and raised it, making her raise her eyes to his. The amber depths were dark with concern, the light of laughter absent.

"I'm listening," she said.

"Good." His gaze searched hers again. "Cass, you are a beautiful and desirable woman. Not just outside, on the inside, too. The idiot who threw you over and broke your heart made you forget that. He made you feel worthless."

She straightened, pride and anger in every line of her body. "I am not. He did not."

"Yes, he did. Hush." He caught her beginning denial and laid a finger across her lips. "He was wrong. He was an idiot. You are everything a man could want and if he couldn't see that, he was blind."

"What does that have to do with you kissing me?"

"Everything." Jason slipped his hands around her waist and lifted her onto his lap, hugging her close. "I kissed you because you're a beautiful, desirable woman and you needed to be reminded."

"So now you're telling me that you kissed me because you

felt sorry for me? What's next, a mercy fuck?"

He answered with a laugh that became a groan. "Sorry is the last thing I feel for you, believe me. But yes, I wanted to soothe your feminine vanity. Why not? I could have just said that I thought you were beautiful and desirable and he was obviously insane, but would it have had the same impact?"

Cass hated to admit it, but it wouldn't have and she knew it. Words were easy to dismiss. Actions spoke louder. He'd kissed her as if his very soul hungered for her and it had more than appeased her wounded vanity.

She sat in silence, wondering how to answer that. Finally, she said, "All right. You've made your point. But that can never happen again."

"Why not?"

"Because I'm a married woman."

"Oh. That."

The teasing irony in his voice made Cass stiffen. "Yes. That."

His arms tightened briefly. "I was kind of hoping you might forget. That scene with the cake and everything."

"Oh, yes. The cake." Feeling somehow lighter, she started to laugh at the reminder. "I wonder where Mona found that cheesecake wedding dress."

"Wedding undress," Jason suggested, joining in her laughter.

"At least she didn't wear the G-string and pearls," Cass pointed out.

"True. It could have been much worse."

"You didn't even look," she accused. "You were watching me instead."

"Yeah, and what a good thing that turned out to be. I

thought you were going to keel right over."

Cass laughed again. "I almost did. Thanks for bringing me outside."

"That's what friends are for."

Yes, that was what friends were for. Jason was proving himself a good friend. But she was enjoying the support and warmth of his embrace too much, and that went past the limits of friendship. She had a husband now, and she had to keep that in mind. He might not be so understanding about their kiss, even if it had happened due to a chain of events that would never be repeated.

She slipped out of Jason's hold and stood. "Well, thank you. I feel much better. I'm so glad the sun finally came out, too."

Jason coughed. "Ah, Uh huh. Sunshine feels good after the rain."

"Mm, it does," Cass agreed, tipping her face up to feel the gentle heat. "Wonderful. Sometimes it seemed like the sun never shone in Seattle."

"Ah, um."

She went on cheerfully, "I'm so glad I moved away from there. Rain, all the time. More than six months out of the year. It gets so depressing."

"Um."

"Yes," Cass said firmly. "Do you know what I want to do? Plant flowers. Plant flowers and watch them grow in the sunshine."

"Um, hmm."

"You probably think that's silly."

"No, no, I wouldn't say silly."

"It's okay, I know it's a girl thing versus a guy thing. I don't

119

expect you to get as excited about the idea of planting petunias as I do."

"That's a relief," he mumbled.

"I wonder if Alex likes flowers. Do you know?"

"Um." Jason coughed. "I'm sure whatever you like will be fine with him."

She brightened. "Do you think so?"

"Sure. Listen, if you're feeling better, do you want to go back inside and have some cake?"

Cass worried her lower lip, debating. She really should go back and say something to Mona. It seemed rude to have run off in the middle of her performance. The woman had been so excited about the wedding and so happy to help that she couldn't believe Mona had meant the spontaneous performance as anything but a gesture of friendship and goodwill.

Decided, she nodded. "Yes, we should get back. Mona might be upset about the way we left."

Jason stared at her, slack-jawed. "She what?"

"Might be upset." Cass frowned at him. "She's gone to a lot of trouble for today. She was trying to help. Her feelings might have been hurt."

"But—but—"

She planted her hands firmly on her hips. "You aren't holding her past against her, are you?"

"No. No, no. But—"

"Then as the proxy groom, you should say something nice to her," Cass stated. "Come on."

She offered him her hand and waited.

He took it and kissed it.

The kiss made the sun seem brighter and the day warmer,

although of course that was ridiculous, not to mention impossible, and if she felt anything at all, it was only gratitude for his friendship. Then he settled her hand in the crook of his arm with a faint shake of his head.

"You, my dear, are a lady," he remarked.

It seemed like a strange thing to say, but he was her new friend, so Cass decided to overlook it. Instead, she smiled at him and patted his arm.

"I'm so glad I have a friend like you," she told him.

If she had been watching, she might have seen his face twist into an expression of agony at the innocent words.

He just kept getting himself in deeper and deeper, he decided. But for the life of him, he couldn't see a way out. The longer he put off telling her, the worse it might be when he finally did.

She'd hardly thank him for his friendship then.

But she was so completely, utterly delightful that how could anyone blame him for putting off the inevitable?

She responded to his needling with flashes of wrath or stiff disapproval that made him want to see her melt and bend. The layer of cool evaporated in a very captivating passion at further needling, making teasing her irresistible.

She had humor and a sweet generosity of spirit.

She also wanted sunshine and flowers, he reminded himself, and wondered how he could cushion the blow when she found out the truth about rainy Ketchikan. For God's sake, they measured rainfall in feet instead of inches. The Liquid Sunshine Gauge that graphically demonstrated their annual rainfall stood more than twice as high as her head.

Still, they did have flowers. Many Alaskan natives thought their short-lived summers produced the most beautiful flowers in the country.

Maybe she'd be consoled by that.

He didn't like the odds, though. A courtship based on deceit and a marriage founded on a lie wouldn't be easy to overlook, even without the problem of explaining to his bride that she'd left Washington's rain for Alaska's.

But he took heart from the way she showed compassion for others, from a homely man to a high-spirited former exotic dancer.

With all that compassion, she might be able to find some to spare for him.

Eventually.

And at least she'd have some positive impressions of him to offset the lies. That would count in his favor, wouldn't it?

It would. Of course it would. She was enjoying his company. She'd enjoyed his kiss. Given a little time, she might come around to seeing that she ought to at least give him a chance.

After all, he hadn't done it on purpose. If she looked at it one way, he'd actually done her a favor, Jason decided magnanimously. He hadn't had to marry her.

But somehow he didn't think she'd see it that way.

Precisely why he wanted to postpone the inevitable telling for as long as possible.

Maybe even forever.

Jason glanced at his new wife and wondered if it could be done.

She caught his look and gave him a sweet smile.

Her smile made his heart nearly stop and the world spin faster. In that moment, he would have given anything, anything at all to see that smile for the rest of his life, just for him.

Then the smile evaporated into concern. "What's wrong?" Cass asked.

I think I love you, he thought. *And before the day is over, you're going to hate me. Other than that, what could be wrong?*

Out loud, he said, "Nothing. Nothing at all."

Lying was really becoming a habit.

But he would do a lot more than lie to keep from losing her smile forever now that he'd seen it.

"Are you sure nothing's wrong?" Cass asked, giving her proxy groom a doubtful look. "I think maybe you're coming down with something. You look green. Maybe you should just go home and go to bed."

An excellent idea. Too bad she didn't plan to join him there.

"Nothing's wrong," he assured her, and resisted the urge to feel his nose to see if it was reflecting the length of his recent lies. Instead, he summoned his reserves of charm. "With a lovely lady like you on my arm, what could possibly be wrong?"

She bit her lower lip and wrinkled her nose in a wry grimace. "You're being so nice about all of this. I'd say plenty has gone wrong. Most men would have run for their lives when a strange woman started crying on them."

"You're not a strange woman," Jason pointed out. "You're my bride."

"For the day," she agreed.

He hoped not.

"By the end of it, I'm sure you'll be glad to hand me over to my rightful husband."

He was her rightful husband. Hand her over? Over his dead body, he would.

"I'm happy to keep an eye on you until Alex shows up," he said, deciding that was a safe statement.

"Well, it's still nice of you. Thank you." With another sweet smile, she leaned up and kissed his cheek.

The innocent brush of her lips across his skin nearly turned him inside-out.

Oh, he was a nice guy, all right, Jason thought in quiet despair.

"When is Alex coming?" Cass asked, looking a little worried. "Sam didn't say."

Jason managed to look surprised. "No? Hmm. Well, I don't know. Maybe we should ask him."

She made a sound of agreement, and he heaved a silent sigh of relief. Safe, for the moment. Another crisis averted.

Abruptly, he stopped and turned her to face him. "Wait. You told me why you wanted to marry Alex, but you didn't tell me why you said you wouldn't marry me."

"Oh." She raised her eyes to his, her face solemn. "It's kind of the same reason. I won't lie to you, Jason, I'm aware that there's a certain chemistry between us."

God, yes. Chemistry didn't begin to describe it. If he ever managed to get inside her, he was pretty sure it would resemble being struck by lightning.

"But that's all it is," she continued. "And I think it's partly due to the unusual circumstances."

He could agree that it would be difficult to imagine more unusual circumstances for two people to meet under, but he wasn't about to go along with the conclusion she drew from that fact.

There was more to it. A lot more.

"We're both adults, not a pair of inexperienced kids to mistake an attraction for more."

"No?" Jason asked. But he thought the wry question failed

to penetrate her brain.

"No."

Was she comparing him to the man who'd broken her heart? "Why?"

She looked a little confused by the intense question, and with an effort, Jason loosened his grip on her shoulders. His fingers had been digging into the flesh without his noticing. He spread his fingers apart and gentled them, stroking her skin in silent apology.

"Because."

He shook his head in exasperation. "I thought we were finally getting beyond that."

She was quiet for a minute. Then she nodded. "You're right. But it isn't easy to put into words. For one thing, you're too good looking."

Of all the things he might have expected her to say, that was the last. His astonishment must have shown on his face, because she looked apologetic.

"I don't mean to hurt your feelings, Jason, but it's true. You're too handsome. I'm tired of dealing with handsome men who think they don't have to make an effort, because so many women fall at their feet and they've never had to try. It's all come too easily. If one woman gets fed up and leaves, another one comes along. But relationships that last aren't easy. I've learned that much. I'm ready to put in the effort and I want a partner who'll do the same."

"Really," he found himself saying.

Cass nodded. "Yes, really. I'm sorry."

"No, I'm sorry. I'm sorry you've decided to let two lowlife jerks convince you that men aren't trustworthy," Jason snarled. He was suddenly unreasonably angry. She wasn't even going to give him a chance? If he lied to her, she had only herself to blame. She wouldn't have even spoken to him if he hadn't.

For a minute, he saw hurt shimmer in her eyes. Then she slipped out of his grasp and went back inside without him, and without saying another word.

Leaving him feeling very alone.

That hadn't gone well. He'd taken offense at her implication that he considered her just another woman and it wouldn't hurt at all if she walked away, because he was all too aware that if he lost her he'd regret the loss of what might have been for the rest of his days. And because he had a guilty conscience. He was lying to her and that meant he could lose her.

He was going to have to come clean. After the spiked punch she'd drunk, she might even listen without throwing something at him, but it would probably go better if he made her some coffee first.

Chapter Eight

Cass forced a bright smile on her face, but inwardly she was consigning one bartender to the nether realms.

She was not allowing the past to dictate the present.

She was not judging all men on the actions of two lowlifes.

She was being practical. Using her head to find the right man. There was a difference.

Of course she was affected by past experience. That couldn't be helped. But it wasn't prejudice that stood between her and Jason, it was reality. And that reality included a gold wedding band. Not to mention the little fact that he was a restless roamer. A gambler. Not the solid, secure, settled sort of husband she was looking for. Attraction wasn't enough to base a life together on, they had to share common goals.

Should she risk her future on the basis of a kiss and a little thing like chemistry? Okay, a big thing, considering the kind of chemistry sizzling between them, but how much of that was him and how much was the situation and the build-up of a year of dull sex or no sex?

She'd be a fool to even consider what he was offering, and her days of being foolish were over.

And even if she took him up on his offer, he'd probably fall all over himself to get out of marrying her, anyway. It wasn't a serious proposal. He was just caught up in chemistry and the romance of playing groom at her wedding. Maybe that was natural, but she wasn't about to let him get so carried away that he'd wreck both of their futures.

Not to mention Alex's.

Making spontaneous, spur-of-the-moment, big risk gestures like that just underscored her point. They were too different.

She needed emotional security, and his risk-taking approach to life would be devastating to live with. Especially since chemistry had a way of wearing off.

It certainly wasn't enough to base a marriage on.

But it had been enough basis for a kiss. A wonderful kiss. A molten lava hot kiss.

Her vaginal walls clenched with need and her clit throbbed just thinking about it, but Cass sternly pushed it out of mind. It was a great memory, everybody should have a kiss like that to remember when they were old, but that was all it was. It belonged in the past.

Alex was her future.

Thinking of Alex had Cass worrying her lower lip once more. Why wasn't he there? Why had she gone through with the wedding without meeting him, without any plans, without even having Lisa there to witness it? She hadn't hit the spiked punch until afterwards so she could only blame it on the man who'd electrified her nerve endings and sent all her plans off kilter.

As if her thoughts had conjured him, he spoke from behind her again.

"You're back to worrying again," Jason said. "See what happens when you wander off without me?"

She turned to glare at him. "Coming up behind me is

128

getting to be a habit with you."

He smiled back at her, unperturbed, and captured her hand to settle it in the crook of his arm again. "If I said it's because you look amazing from behind, you wouldn't like it. So let's just put it down to one of my eccentricities. Come on. I'll introduce you around," he offered.

She hesitated.

"Come on," he coaxed, as if reading her thoughts. "It's the least I can do. I'm sorry I upset you again."

"All right." Giving in, she followed him as he headed towards a group of people. Even as she told herself that she didn't need to defend herself to him, she found herself saying, "And you're wrong. I don't think all men are untrustworthy."

"No?"

She met his eyes steadily, ignoring the devilish light that said he was needling her again. "No."

"Only gamblers, is that it?"

"Exactly."

Jason gave her a sharp look at that sweet comment, but she ignored it and made a slight gesture towards the nearest member of the group. "Who's this?"

She thought she could feel him grinding his teeth before he gave up and followed through on his offer to introduce her. But he got even with her by shifting from guiding her by a hand on his arm to guiding her by a hand on her waist.

Cass pretended not to notice that the intimate, possessive gesture made her intensely aware of his presence and his touch. At least, she pretended for about five minutes that seemed eternal and then she couldn't take it anymore.

"Your hand," she muttered to him, smiling through clenched teeth for the rest of the crowd to see. "Move it."

He stroked her waist. "Like that?"

God. That molten lava feeling was back and she was going to go Vesuvius on him if she didn't put some distance between them, and fast. "Stop it. Now."

She pulled away and then realized that she'd been free to move all along. She'd just been too distracted by the electric touch of his hand on her bare skin and the hungry heat building inside her core to think.

Just like she'd been too distracted and rushed to think about what was happening to her and around her all day, but she was paying attention now and a lot of little things were starting to add up.

She took a deep breath, counted to ten, and let it out slowly. "Is this day over? Because I really think I need it to be over."

"You and me both."

"Good. Take me home, please."

"Done."

Jason took her arm again before she could move it out of his reach and guided her out and away, making excuses and saying goodbyes.

She didn't say another word and neither did he, not on the way to the car, not on the drive, not until they were inside what must be his bar overlooking the water. On top of the water, actually. The historic buildings on Creek Street didn't have basements, but they had great views.

She saw Rex in a corner on his dog bed, sleeping off the last of his travel drugs. He seemed to have made himself right at home there, she noted. She perched on a bar stool while Jason went around behind the bar and started a pot of coffee brewing for her. He poured a glass of seltzer water for himself.

When the coffee had brewed enough, he poured out a mug and slid it across the bar to her. She put her hands in her lap instead of reaching for it. The liquid would be hot and she didn't quite trust herself with it.

"Thank you for getting us out of there. I didn't want to have the first screaming fight of our marriage in front of all those witnesses," Cass said.

He set his glass down and stared at her. "Excuse me?"

She stared right back at him. "When were you going to tell me?"

He leaned forward and placed his hands on her shoulders in a firm grip, as if he was worried that she'd bolt. Ha. She wasn't going anywhere until they had this out. And then, well, they'd see.

"I was going to tell you, but I thought it might be best to have that conversation in private. For obvious reasons. And I thought I should make you some coffee first, in case the punch was still affecting your judgment." He studied her face, not at all discomfited by her deduction but with a lot of interest. "What gave it away?"

"I read a lot of nonfiction," she said.

"That would explain why the grout article had you so fascinated. You wanted some nice calm facts to fix your mind on during the trip instead of worrying about marrying a mystery man."

Ignoring him, she went on, "Last year I read a book called *Blink*. It's about how most of the thinking we do we never know we do. Little cues that we process and store away and aren't consciously aware of. And we use this information we don't know we have to make all sorts of decisions."

"Sounds right."

"There were a lot of little cues and I started to think about them." Cass started to tick them off, one by one.

"You came to meet me in Seattle and you talked to me like you knew me. You were trying to get a rise out of me, but you were too accurate with your shots. Sam and Mona and everybody else fell all over themselves to make this happen fast, before I could back out, and they were all happy for you. Not for somebody who wasn't there. You. They looked at us together like they approved, and like they had something to do with it. You kissed me like you had a right to and I kissed you back the same way."

She realized as she said it she was now staring at his mouth. She jerked her attention away from it before it distracted her and focused on his eyes again. "That was the biggest clue, I think. That wasn't a sneaking around kind of kiss. That and the way you were always touching me was like some kind of body language branding that said *my woman.* So why didn't you just tell me it was you?"

Cass really tried not to, but she ended on a near-scream. Maybe she needed to count to ten once more. Or maybe to one hundred. She really didn't want to start throwing things at him when she might regret it later.

"You didn't seem very impressed with me in person, for starters," Jason pointed out.

"I'm less impressed that you made up Alex. What was behind that?"

He started to answer, stopped and shook his head. "You want answers. You're entitled to them. And I will give them to you. But first, I want to make you an offer."

"I'm listening."

He took both of her arms, tracing his hands along her skin, up to her shoulders. "Do you feel that?"

She started to laugh in spite of herself. "Is that a joke? I'm out of practice but I'm not dumb."

Jason smiled at her. "I never thought you were." Then his face went serious. "We get one chance at creating the memory of our wedding night. I don't want to look back on tonight and remember how much I wanted to be with you and instead I spent the night on the couch. Tomorrow I will tell you anything you want to know. I will answer every question. I will explain the picture, everything. Tonight, I want you."

The hell of it was, she wanted him, too. And even though she knew he'd lied to her, she trusted him. It was beyond dumb, but there was probably some subliminal cue that made her believe she could trust him.

Of course, it could also be the way he was touching her and the dud year of sex she suddenly wanted to make up for. If there ever was a man who could make up for a dud year of sex, it was the one in front of her.

Figuring action spoke louder and words had only gotten them in trouble so far anyway, Cass stripped off her shirt, tossed it on the bar, and followed it with her bra before she lost her nerve.

"That looks like yes." Jason pulled her up onto the bar and she cooperated by climbing up to meet him. He drew her forward, facing him. Her legs fell to either side of his body as he drew her closer, until she was balanced on the edge of the bar with him standing between her legs.

She felt him reach for something she couldn't see and then he slid a brightly decorated gift bag across the bar top until it touched her hip. "Mona gave us a present," he said. "I'm guessing there will be condoms in here."

Cass tipped the bag over and let the contents spill free.

There were condoms. In a range of flavors. Gel that heated

when applied to skin. Two kinds of lubricant, one non-vaginal. A Bad Boy vibrator. Handcuffs. A pink flogger. Three sort-of-jeweled clips with dangling beads that weren't earrings and that Cass had no idea what to do with but Jason probably did.

No matter what else happened after tonight, one thing was clear. Her year of dud sex was officially over.

"Dear God."

She caught Jason's expression of horror as he stared at the items scattered on the bar top beside her and giggled. "I guess that means you don't want to take turns with the little whip?"

"I think we can skip that one, yes."

"Oh, I don't know." She picked it up and flicked it experimentally. "You've been bad. Lying to me. Maybe you should be spanked."

Jason plucked it out of her grasp and hid it underneath the bar. "Maybe you shouldn't mix alcohol with bondage and discipline."

"Does that mean you don't want to play with these, either?" Cass scooped up the handcuffs and dangled them in front of him.

"Maybe." He took them from her and turned them in his hands, examining them. "Hmm. They don't look dangerous." Jason snapped one over her wrist, tugged it behind her back, and cuffed her other hand. "How does that feel?"

Cass looked down at herself. She was naked from the top down, seated on a bar, her hands cuffed behind her back, with a man who was a virtual stranger standing between her open thighs. "Pretty damn kinky."

"Anything else?"

She licked her lips, suddenly aware of her nipples hardening into two tight buds, her sex growing swollen and slick, and waves of heat rippling through her body. "Hot."

Jason's eyes went darker. "I meant, did they pinch or feel uncomfortable. But if they make you hot, we'll keep them."

"Okay." She should have felt silly sitting there wearing nothing but handcuffs on her upper half, but all she felt was turned on.

"You look fantastic," Jason told her. "You also look delicious."

His eyes moved down to her breasts and Cass felt her nipples throb with need. She literally ached for him to touch her.

He picked up the gel and frowned over the instructions. "Gets hot when you blow on it," he read out loud. He gave her an enquiring look. "Feeling adventurous? Want to find out if this makes you hotter?"

Her breath caught in her throat and she thought she felt her heart flip over. Playing. He was playing with her. How long had it been since she'd played in bed? When had a man last made her hot and made her laugh and made her want to scream?

Cass realized he was waiting for an answer. He wouldn't test the gel unless she wanted him to. She knew he wouldn't do anything she didn't want him to, and that meant she could relax and play with him, surrender to the moment and enjoy herself.

She was suddenly very eager to play. "Yes. I'm feeling adventurous. Try it on my nipples."

Jason shook his head. "Let's test it on a less sensitive spot first. If you like it, we'll move on from there." He uncapped it and let a drop fall into the valley between her breasts. Then he lowered his head to her skin and breathed against the gel.

Oh. Heat flared over her skin and she felt her breasts tighten. He licked the sensitized skin and she shivered. His mouth brushed against the curves of her breasts, but didn't go farther.

Cass would have grabbed his head and directed him to her nipples if her hands had been free. Since they weren't, she let out a low sound of frustration and shifted her torso, trying to guide him where she wanted him to go.

Jason raised his head and looked into her eyes. "Not too hot?"

"God, yes, I'm on fire," she informed him. Then her head cleared enough for her to understand his meaning. "Oh, you mean the gel. No, it's not too hot. Try it on my nipples now."

He let a drop fall onto each nipple, and Cass gasped at the sensation. Then she closed her eyes and let her head fall back while he blew across each peak, sending heat rolling down to throb between her legs. His mouth closed over one nipple and the throb increased in intensity. She needed pressure there. Right now.

Cass raised her legs and locked them around his hips, pressing her swollen, needy sex against the bulge of his erection. They were wearing too many clothes, she thought vaguely, but this was a step in the right direction.

Jason rocked his hips into the cradle of her pelvis and ground, giving her pressure right where she wanted it. "Yes," she moaned. "God, that feels good."

His mouth tugged on her nipples, first one, then the other, traveling over the sensitive skin between, and it made her feel nearly crazed combined with the heat and pressure of his cock between her legs.

He kissed his way between her breasts and down, over the curve of her belly, and stopped at the waistband of her jeans.

"Don't stop," Cass urged. "Take them off."

He let out a low laugh against the soft skin of her belly. "Not yet. Are you always this bossy in bed?"

"We're not in bed. I'm sitting on top of your bar," Cass pointed out. Then she frowned. "I'm not bossy." At least, she hadn't been before. She didn't remember ever urging Tom to hurry. She remembered more than once wishing he'd take more time.

"Maybe we need to establish who's the boss right now. I think it's the one who has the key to the handcuffs." Jason grinned at her and reached for one of the little clips. "Do you know what this is for?"

"No idea," she informed him cheerfully. "Does it have instructions?"

"I don't need instructions."

Cass arched her back in a luxurious stretch, feeling sensual and relaxed and playful and incredibly turned on all at once. "Yep. You're a man."

"I'm a man who is wise in the ways of the world." He winked at her and attached the little piece of jewelry to her nipple. "Tell me when it's tight enough. It should pinch just a little but not hurt."

"Oh." She relaxed while he adjusted the fit until she said, "There."

What an idea. Jewelry to stimulate her nipples with. Strippers knew about the most interesting things. "Remind me to write Mona a very nice thank you letter," Cass said.

"Thank you letter, hell. I plan to buy her a cruise ticket." Jason attached the second clip to her nipple and adjusted the pressure to match the first. "Do you have any idea how hot you look wearing those?"

Cass looked. He was right, she did look hot. Exotic. Erotic. Sprawling on top of a bar counter, the little clips on her nipples drawing attention to them while stimulating them, her hands cuffed behind her back. "I should wear these all the time. I look like a sex goddess." She looked over at the selection of toys on the bar beside her and asked, "What's the third one for?"

"Your clit." Jason settled his hand over her mound and squeezed. "It might be too much."

It might make her come the instant he put it on her, Cass thought. "Let's try it."

"Later." He massaged her sex through her jeans while he looked down at her. "Right now, I want to touch you."

Oh. Good plan. Cass decided to cooperate with it. "Please do."

"I want to take you pants off, Cass, and then I want to look and touch and taste."

All the air left her lungs. She nodded her consent and felt a tremor wrack her when he undid her jeans and worked them over her hips and off. He stripped her from the waist down, leaving her naked except for the little jeweled clips on her nipples and the handcuffs behind her back. It was decadent and exciting and she wanted him to look and touch and taste.

"Spread your legs wide open for me, Cass."

She obeyed. It felt like something out of a dream. An erotic dream that she didn't want to wake up from.

"My God, you're beautiful." Jason traced a finger the length of her sex, then worked it between the folds. "And so hot." His finger thrust inside her and Cass gasped. "So wet." His voice went low and husky with desire.

"I want to taste you, Cass. I want to put my mouth on you."

"*Yes.*"

His mouth closed over her clit. He sucked the sensitive bundle of nerves while he slid a second finger into her and Cass let out a low moan of pleasure

Jason released her, reached for the third clip and applied it carefully to her sensitized clit. She missed the penetration of his fingers instantly. Then the light pressure of the clip made her eyes widen.

The delicate clips on her nipples made them throb and the throbbing sensation between her legs built. The decorative beads from all three clips dangled and brushed sensitive skin, making her shiver. She was in a heightened state of awareness and arousal when Jason's clever mouth and hands returned to tease her.

His tongue flicked over her sex while his fingers worked in and out of her. She felt her muscles clench and knew she was going to come seconds before the orgasm hit. She felt it swell and build and then release in a rush of pleasure while her sex clamped down on his fingers.

"Oh," she gasped. "Oh, I needed that."

"Has it been a long time?"

"Yes. A while. And before that, you know. Not much." Cass stretched, feeling satisfied and still very aroused at the same time. "Nothing like this. These things are amazing."

"Not as amazing as me." His tongue thrust into her sex and Cass gasped.

"No, not as amazing as you," she agreed.

He licked and sucked at her while the clips tantalized her.

"Jason. I need more. I need you inside me."

"So demanding." He stripped his clothes off and reached for one of the packets of condoms. "We have a problem, though."

"What?" Cass practically screamed. He couldn't possibly

mean to stop now. She'd kill him.

"This bar, it's the wrong height." He ripped opened the packet and rolled the condom on, tossed the package behind him and helped her down. "And if I try to make it up the stairs with you, I'm going to come just from watching you walk, with your bare ass swishing in front of me and your hands cuffed above it."

Cass felt her mouth twitch. "I don't swish."

"Your ass is an invitation." He carried her over to a table and arranged her on it so that she was seated on the edge with her cuffed hands behind her bracing her upright. He stepped between her legs, and let his cock nudge against the slick, softened folds of her sex. "Are you ready for this?"

"I'll kill you if you don't fuck me now."

Jason laughed. "You'll have to wait until I set you free. You're helpless in those handcuffs."

"I'm dangerous," Cass informed him. "Don't mess with me. Give me what I want."

"Always." Jason gripped her hips and began to thrust into her. "Tell me if it hurts, if you need the third clip off."

"Ah. I think it's in the way."

"Right." He pulled back and removed the piece of jewelry. Then he looked at her, seated on the edge of the table, naked, legs spread. "Where were we?"

"Do me now or die."

"I choose life." He entered her in a slow, sure stroke until he was seated fully inside her. Cass sighed in relief and pleasure as she felt him filling her, her sex stretching to take him. He waited for her to adjust, then asked, "Comfortable?"

"Um." She bit lightly at his shoulder and felt him shudder. "Yes. Except for one thing."

"What?"

"You're not moving."

"I'm going to make sure that whip never falls into your hands." Jason kissed her forehead and began to move in and out with slow, deep thrusts.

Cass felt his cock slide against the most sensitive spot and arched into him. "Yes. There. *Ohhh.*"

She was going to come again, already. He was so hard and hot inside her, filling her, the fit so perfect. Jason increased the tempo, making his strokes shorter and harder, each one ending against that point, giving her pressure right where she needed it. "Jason," she whispered, her breath ragged.

"Now?"

"Yes."

He rocked into her hard and fast and as the first tremors of orgasm hit her, she felt his cock swelling and throbbing inside her from his release. It intensified the sensation of her own rippling pleasure and Cass bucked against him, lost in the moment.

Afterwards he leaned into her and wrapped his arms around her, giving her the support of his torso to rest against. She felt him drop a kiss on top of her head. Then he reached down and pressed a button, releasing the catch on the handcuffs.

"I thought you said you had the key," Cass said.

"This kind doesn't have a key. Probably safer that way. Imagine if it got lost." Jason took the opened cuffs off her wrists and dropped them onto the table next to the erotic clip.

He was probably right about that. Cass stretched her arms and then wrapped them around him, snuggling into him while he stood between her legs, his cock still buried inside her. The clips she wore exerted just enough pressure on her nipples while the dangling beads teased the sensitive skin of her breasts. Cass was pretty sure if she kept them on, the stimulation would have her ready for another round of sex in minutes.

"Sleepy?"

She yawned involuntarily and then laughed at her response. "I guess I am."

"Hmm. Maybe you should be in bed."

He ground his pelvis into hers suggestively and Cass laughed again. "Maybe I should. Are you going to tuck me in?"

"I was thinking of something that rhymed with tuck." Jason withdrew and Cass felt suddenly empty. He took her hands and helped her off the table, scooped up the clip and handcuffs and led her over to the bar where he tossed the condom into the trash and gathered everything else back into the bag they'd emptied earlier. "Can't leave this stuff lying around down here," he informed her. "Somebody might have a coronary."

Cass felt her lips twitch. "It would be hard to explain."

"I think it's self-explanatory." Jason flicked the beads that dangled from one nipple, making them dance over her breast. "Hot woman. Hot toys. But I don't intend to give any of the lonely bachelors around here ideas, unless it involves finding their own woman. Come on."

He held the bag in one hand and placed the other on the small of her back, guiding her. Cass followed, letting the light pressure and the heat of his hand on her bare skin indicate the way.

"We live upstairs," Jason informed her. "The bar's downstairs."

"We?"

"Positive thinking. Also, I have handcuffs. Those might come in really handy when I tell you the tale of how I went fishing online in the personal ads," he mused.

"There's also that whip," Cass muttered, but without any real heat. She was too relaxed right now and maybe it was the rosy haze of afterglow from two very satisfying orgasms after a very dry year, but she couldn't help feeling positive right along with Jason. She tried to picture herself living here. "You know, there's something about this place. All the red and gold. Who did the interior design?"

"Ah. Well, Creek Street has a history." Jason coughed. "Okay, well, The Last Resort is a former bordello. This place once housed fallen women."

Cass looked down at herself, naked except for nipple jewelry. "It still does, apparently. I seem to have fallen."

"I'll catch you."

She smiled at his solemn promise. "Before or after I hit the mattress?"

"Before, after, during. I'm flexible." He tugged her through a doorway and guided her over to a king-sized bed. "Try falling on that one, we'll see what works best."

"It looks comfortable." Cass looked from the bed to him, backed up to it until she felt it against her legs, and let herself fall.

Chapter Nine

The mattress was softer than she expected. Cass sank into it. "Hm. Nice," she told Jason.

He looked down at her, his eyes dark. "Naughty."

He set the bag on the mattress and climbed onto the bed, kneeling over her. "Are these starting to bother you?" He brushed the beads that dangled over her breasts with his fingers.

"I think I've probably worn them long enough for a first timer," she decided.

Jason removed the clips from her nipples and dropped them into the bag. Then he filled his hands with her breasts. She sighed as he kneaded and stroked, soothing and stimulating her flesh at the same time. His hands felt warm, electric and so right. It was hard to believe they hadn't been doing this for years.

"That's strange," she said out loud.

"Perfectly normal," he said, caressing her nipples. "You have breasts, I'm touching them. The nipple clips, those were unusual."

Cass laughed. "That's not what I meant. It's strange that we're so comfortable with each other. Sex isn't usually like this."

"How is it usually? For you?" He looked into her eyes, his face serious.

"Well, not bad or anything. Just, well. Not all that exciting. And not..." Her voice trailed off for a minute. "The first time with somebody, it's usually kind of awkward. You know. Not quite getting things right, off rhythm. Like bumping noses when you go to kiss, but more so."

"Maybe they just weren't very in tune with you." Jason leaned down and kissed her. She let her eyes drift closed and her lips moved against his, enjoying the light pressure and the warmth of his mouth.

"That's exactly what I mean," she said when the kiss ended. "No bumped noses. Like we've been practicing this."

"I'm willing to practice." Jason released her breasts and rolled to lie beside her. He hooked one leg over hers and settled a hand on her belly. "But I understand your point. I think you can put it down to a combination of chemistry, affinity and paying attention."

He moved his hand in a slow line along her torso, up to the bottom curve of her breasts, down to the top of her mound. Cass shifted, letting her legs part slightly in invitation. His hand moved lower, cupping her mound, sliding between her legs. "Like that," he said. "You let me know you'd like me to touch you there. I paid attention."

"I'm certainly paying attention," she sighed. Her eyes drifted shut and she cuddled into him. "For instance, I noticed that we do not need a mechanical Bad Boy substitute to compensate for anything."

"You never know, you might want to save that for a rainy day," he teased.

Cass made a face. "Don't say that. I'm leaving the rain behind."

145

Jason coughed.

Cass opened her eyes. "What?"

He looked down at her. "You know, it does rain here."

She stared at him. "We just had bondage sex in a public bar. We're naked. Your hand is between my legs, and you want to talk about the weather?"

"No. But you brought it up."

She didn't think she had, but it was too much trouble to replay the conversation. "Let's get back to the important stuff. Like what your hand is doing down there. Much more interesting than a weather report."

Cass felt him circle the sensitive nub of her clit with his finger. "Very interesting," he agreed. "I think the forecast is for wet."

She giggled, and then sighed as he stroked and fondled her sex. "You're right." Then she stirred. "Hey. What about you?"

"What about me?"

"I'm the one on the receiving end here. That doesn't seem fair." Cass rolled onto her side, facing him and let one hand roam the expanse of his chest.

"Maybe tonight isn't about fair." Jason captured her hand and kissed it.

"What's it about, then?"

"Love and war." He rolled her onto her back and pinned her with his body.

"Feels more like naked wrestling to me." Cass wrapped her legs around his, twisted underneath him and attempted to reverse their positions. When she didn't succeed, she sank her nails into his butt and laughed when he reacted.

"Not fair."

"I thought everything was fair." She gave him an innocent look.

"So you want to play rough?" He grinned at her and captured her wrists in his hands, pinning them above her head. He shifted position in the process and Cass felt his cock slide against her sex. The contact made her lose her breath.

"Cass." Jason looked into her eyes and moved again, sliding against her deliberately. She let him see her reaction, the heat in her eyes, her lips parting. "I was planning to go slower the second time. Keep looking at me like that and it's going to be over in a few minutes."

The idea of making him lose control, making him come, made Cass turn liquid. She rolled her hips under him, sliding his cock along her sex with her motion. He groaned. "Stop that."

"Make me." Her voice sounded throaty, sexy. Not at all practical.

Jason levered himself up and flipped her onto her belly, then covered her with his body before she could move. His cock nestled against her butt. "There. Got you now."

Cass rocked her hips again, knowing that riding his erection along the crease between her buttocks wasn't going to help him at all.

He groaned. She laughed, helpless to stop, rolling her hips under him again and delighting in the feel of him hard and hot against her.

"Okay, you win," Jason conceded. "Fast now. Slow later."

She heard him fumbling and guessed he was digging out another condom. A tearing sound confirmed her guess. He shifted away from her and then tugged at her hips with his hands. "Up on your knees."

Cass pushed herself onto her hands and knees and felt the

blunt head of his cock pressing against her opening. She moved back against Jason, forcing the head inside her. He held her hips in a firm grip and thrust home, filling her with one long stroke. It felt so good, but she needed so much more. "Jason," she whispered.

"I'm right here." He leaned over her and kissed her back. "Tell me what you need."

"I need you, hard and fast inside me," she said through dry lips. "Pound me."

His hands flexed on her hips. "We're in a good position for that, but I could also bump your cervix and that might hurt." Jason pushed forward, driving himself even deeper inside her. "How does that feel?"

"Good," she groaned. "More."

He started off slowly, giving her long, deep strokes that ended with his cock buried as far inside her as he could go. When she only pushed back against him to meet his thrusts and take him even deeper, he sped up, giving her the pounding she'd asked for after making sure she could take it.

"Yes, Jason," she gasped, "Harder. I need it harder." The tension coiling in her belly was more than she could take. Need thrummed through every nerve ending. He slammed into her hard and fast, pounding her sex, impaling her with his cock, and Cass felt her muscles clench and then spasm around him as she came with a muffled shriek.

He came with her, burying himself inside her with one last thrust, his cock jerking. "Cass."

"Jason." She was gasping for breath, her arms shaking from exertion. She collapsed face-down on the bed, unable to keep herself up, and Jason moved with her, blanketing her with his body, his hands coming up to brace on either side of her shoulders.

"Hey." He pulled out of her and turned on his side, pulling her close. "I've got you."

He certainly did, Cass thought. She curled into him, feeling limp and spent. His arms closed around her, his chest made a pillow for her cheek, and his heart thundered against her ear. She felt protected. Possessed. And a little embarrassed. Had that been her talking? *Pound me, harder?* What did he think of her now?

He kissed her forehead and smoothed her hair along her back. "You were right. Plenty of time for slow later." He hugged her and added, "I think."

"You think?"

"We might not manage to slow down tonight and you might not want to try it with me at any speed tomorrow. Or the next day."

"Am I really going to hate what you have to tell me?" Cass asked cautiously.

"I think we can safely say you won't like it." His arms tightened around her. "Am I wrong in thinking that you like me?"

She breathed him in and felt the ache he'd left between her thighs. "I like you."

"Good. Because no matter what happens, I want you to understand that I don't intend to let you get away."

Cass pressed her face against his chest, not wanting to look into his eyes just now. She didn't want to think about the past or the future. She didn't want to be confronted with unpleasant truths. Tonight was a fantasy and she wanted it.

She thought of what she knew of this man so far. She knew he was a considerate lover. The chemistry between them was explosive, yet he'd taken each step slowly, making sure she was ready for it, checking her reaction to everything from how the handcuffs felt to how deep she could comfortably take penetration.

People revealed themselves in bed. Matthew hadn't cared about her pleasure, except in terms of how it made him look. If she didn't come, he wasn't a stud. After a while it had started to feel like pressure to perform for the sake of his ego's gratification more than mutual satisfaction.

Tom...Cass tried to imagine doing it doggy style with Tom and asking him to pound her with his cock. Even in her imagination, it couldn't happen. That was too primal, too sweaty, too uninhibited.

That word clicked in her mind like a key turning. She was uninhibited with Jason, as if she was safe to be her full self, to say or do anything she wanted to. If she wanted him to handcuff her and put clamps on her nipples and fuck her as hard as she could take it, he was happy to oblige. He seemed perfectly at home living in a former bordello.

Tom would have been horrified.

"You okay?" Jason tugged at her hair gently, prompting her to look up at him.

"Yes." She tilted her head up and met his eyes. "Just thinking."

"That could be dangerous." His lips quirked with humor.

"I was thinking everybody deserves to have this."

"What, a bagful of naughty toys from Santa's X-rated elves?"

Cass shook her head. "No. Somebody to use them with."

His smile vanished and she saw something in his eyes. Something hot and deep. "Cass." He tugged her head closer with his hands in her hair, drawing her into his kiss. His mouth took hers so thoroughly her lips felt branded when he finally raised his head.

She stared into his eyes, at a loss for words. No matter what happened tomorrow, tonight he'd done something she never expected, hadn't realized she needed. "I always thought it was a bunch of crap," she said without thinking.

"Excuse me?" His brows arced up.

"That whole validating your experience thing pop psychologists are always going on about. I always found myself thinking if you want validation, you buy something and get your parking ticket stamped. You don't get it from a relationship. Except I do from my friends. And now you."

"Explain that, please." His eyes burned into hers.

"This. Tonight." Cass closed her eyes and took a breath, trying to put it into words. "I was being myself with you. My sexual self. And you liked it. And you were yourself with me. Not performing, not planning the next big deal. Just being you, with me." She opened her eyes, feeling suddenly naked and needing to see that he understood.

He did. She saw it in his eyes. And more.

He touched her lower lip with one finger. "Stay with me and you can have that every night."

"What about days?" Cass nipped at his finger and he smiled at her.

"They last a long time during certain points of the year." His eyebrows wiggled meaningfully. "And so do the nights. I do have a business to run, but we can always hire a backup bartender to take over if you need a quickie in the middle of work hours."

Cass laughed and tried to picture that. She sobered as she realized it was all too easy to imagine. Coming down to the bar, giving Jason a look that he would instantly understand. He'd make an excuse and follow her, and they would fall on each other. Mouths meeting, tongues tangling. Hands touching, holding, unbuttoning and unzipping and discarding clothing that got in the way. And then Jason, hard and hot inside her.

She blinked and gave her head a shake to clear it. "I have to work too, you know."

"Planning to do shifts in the bar?" He smiled.

"No, shooting tourists."

Jason shook his head at her. "I know they call it tourist season, but that's no reason to try to bag your limit. Tourism is our biggest industry, next to fish. We frown on shooting them. Makes it hard for them to come back next year or recommend Ketchikan to their friends."

"With my camera." Cass grinned at him. "I got a gig with a fishing charter, taking pictures of the tourists with their trophy catches when they come back in. It's a souvenir. I'll also be taking nature shots for stock photography sales, and I was thinking about doing more freelance work, too."

"That's right, you're a photographer." He rolled onto his back and tugged her up onto his chest. His hands traced lazy patterns along her spine.

"Uh huh. I want to work up to full-time but I'm not quite there yet. I do a lot of freelance work and my stock photography sales are pretty steady. But it's not enough to live on, so that's why I took the fishing photo job. It'll keep steady money coming in and pay for my more artistic endeavors." Cass snuggled into him and shifted to sprawl in a more comfortable position.

"You like to do art photography? You never mentioned that."

"I didn't?" Cass thought about the emails they'd written and realized neither of them had been very specific about what they did, focusing more on what they wanted in a relationship. "Sorry. I should have. Writing felt so awkward, it was hard to know what to say." She pointed at his chest. "You didn't say what you did, either. Local business owner is about all you told me, I think."

"Let's forget I brought up the emails," Jason said. He ran his hands through her hair. "But I'm glad to know more about you. Tell me about your art."

"I like to experiment, especially with portraits. People make such fascinating subjects. Know what I'd really love?"

"What?"

"A Holga."

"What's that?" Jason asked. "Some incredibly expensive piece of equipment?"

Cass laughed and stretched, sliding her leg along his in the process, enjoying the feel of his body against hers. "No. It's the cheapest camera made. It leaks light. Every Holga is unique and that's what makes it interesting. The images are one of a kind, you can get all sorts of amazing effects from one. And it's the least expensive medium format camera you can get."

"How inexpensive?"

"Fifteen to twenty dollars," she told him, grinning at the very idea of taking serious art shots with what was essentially a plastic toy.

"That little? So why don't you have one already?"

"For the same reason I've never made a pinhole camera." She sighed. "The artsy stuff is time-consuming and you can spend a fortune on film and processing, which gets hard to justify. Then there's time. My time is always at a premium. If I have some to spare, I usually put it towards work I know I can sell and not experimentation."

She was really looking forward to the day when she could afford to experiment the way she wanted to, in terms of both time and money. Thanks to Jason, that day wasn't far off.

"Usually?" Jason tugged at her hair until she lifted her head to look at him.

"Usually." She smiled and traced a random pattern on his shoulder. "My friend Lisa posed for lots of experimental portraiture shots. Good practice for me, and it's let me slowly build up a portfolio of the kind of work I want to do more of in the future."

"What about your nature photography for stock?"

"That's art, too, but different." Cass propped her chin on his chest. "More impersonal. Portraiture can be very intimate, revealing the subject's personality and emotions. Trees and mountains are beautiful, but not very emotional. They don't respond to the camera or the photographer and they don't have moods."

"I never thought of photography as something emotional."

"With any art form, the goal is to provoke an emotional response," Cass said. "Anger, laughter, sentimental warmth, it should make you feel something."

"I feel something," Jason said. "You're provoking me."

"I'm just lying here."

"You're lying there naked. That's very provocative, even if you weren't on my bed and I hadn't just been inside you and this wasn't our wedding night."

Cass peered at him. "Did you have a lot of that punch?"

"I never drink." He gave her a half smile. "But you pack a wallop."

"I do, huh?" She considered the idea that she could be having an impact on him equal to the one he had on her. "Do I

154

make you feel warm and kind of tingly and lightheaded and extremely satisfied but hungry for more at the same time?"

"Yes," Jason toyed with her hair. "Although now that you mention it, I'm hungry for something besides your delicious self. What about you? When did you last eat?"

"I don't remember," Cass said, thinking back. "Breakfast?"

"No wonder you keeled over at the wedding." He gave her a light kiss. "Not enough food, too much punch and too many surprises."

"Not all the surprises were unwelcome," Cass said, thinking of the chemistry between them, which she'd hoped to find with the fictitious Alex, the bag of naughty surprises Mona had gifted them with, and Jason's very skillful use of the contents of that bag.

"Still. It's a lot to absorb. You need some food to cushion all those shocks to your system."

Jason inside her had definitely been a shock to her system, but in a very good way, Cass decided. Then her stomach growled, proving that he had a point. "Food does sound good," she said. "Which way is the kitchen?"

He smiled at her. "I'd say come with me, but you already did." His smile widened when she blushed. "If you'll let me up, now that you've used my body to satisfy your lust, I'll lead the way."

Cass rolled away and then stood up. Once on her feet, she suddenly felt naked. With a man she barely knew. She felt herself blushing even darker. Jason noticed and tugged her into his arms.

"Hey. What happened to the shameless wanton who wanted me to handcuff her and pound her harder?"

Cass groaned and buried her face in his shoulder. "Oh,

God."

"Don't start thinking of me as a stranger now," he said. He ran his hands down her back and settled them intimately over the curve of her backside. "I've been inside you. I plan to do it again. I'm looking forward to doing it again."

His cock twitched against her bare belly, silent testament to the truth of that statement. "It's a little awkward," she pointed out. "I just met you."

"Hell of an introduction." Jason squeezed her butt. "And no, I don't think you make a habit of meeting men and jumping straight into the sack. I think we can agree that everything about our situation is an exception."

That was putting it mildly. Cass nodded her agreement.

"Now you're tired and hungry, so as much as I like looking at you naked, I'll find you a tee shirt to wear and I'll put on some shorts, and we'll go raid the kitchen. Okay?"

"Okay." When he set her away, she missed the warmth of his body against hers and the comfort of his arms around her. He found a shirt for her, one of his, and pulled it over her head, then directed her arms through the sleeves.

"There." He dropped a kiss on her forehead before turning away to pull on a pair of shorts.

Cass noted that he'd skipped underwear and he wasn't offering her anything else to put on under her shirt, either. By his actions he was telling her that this was just an intermission in what promised to be one unforgettable night of sex, and not the end of it.

That warmed her all over, and when he reached out to take her hand, twining his fingers with hers, the warmth reached all the way to her center and made her glow.

Her mail-order bride plan was working. She'd gotten

married in time, secured her inheritance, and unless she was very wrong about Jason, she just might have gotten everything else she wanted, too.

A little worry nibbled at her, but she ignored it. She could find out what was behind the false name and the false picture tomorrow. Tonight, she wanted to believe in happily ever after.

Chapter Ten

The kitchen raid wasn't so much an organized strike as a meandering, post-coital browse after stopping on the way to take turns in the bathroom. Jason got out plates while Cass peered into the refrigerator, taking in the options. "I see a lot of pizza here," she said.

"Pizza is the perfect food. It covers all the essential nutritional groups, and you can get it delivered."

Cass turned to look at Jason over her shoulder. "Does this mean I married a man who can't cook?"

"I can cook." He gave her a lazy smile. "Maybe nothing too advanced, but I can handle the basics. I just don't always take the time to cook for myself." He walked over to wrap an arm around her waist and hug her from behind. "Don't worry, I didn't marry you to get free domestic help. I expect to do my share."

Cass thought about asking him why he had married her the way he had, with speed and subterfuge, then decided it fell into the category of things she didn't really want to know tonight. Better to stick to the subject at hand. "Good to know. Domestic chores are a fact of life, but my world doesn't revolve around them."

"How about sex?" Jason nuzzled the curve of her neck. "Does your world revolve around that?"

"If you keep doing that, it could happen," Cass admitted. "I might turn into a crazed sex addict, demanding it night and day."

"If you get too demanding, I can always tame you with the handcuffs, the flogger and the vibrator." He nibbled at the sensitive line of neck and shoulder and Cass felt her breasts growing heavy in response.

"I'm not sure I want to know how you'd use that combination to tame me," she said. But the image had sprung to vivid, Technicolor life in her head. She could picture herself, naked, her hands cuffed behind her, kneeling while Jason came at her with those sexual weapons in his hands, giving her a knowing look that said *I'm going to take charge and you're going to enjoy yourself.*

Her legs were starting to feel a little weak, so she leaned back against him and let him partially support her.

"Your nipples just got harder," Jason murmured. "I think you'd like to try that combination out."

"It's the cold air from the refrigerator," Cass said, knowing full well that he'd recognize the blatant lie. Her sex clenched and she shifted, pressing her thighs together.

"Feels like it's getting hot in here to me." The arm he'd wrapped around her moved, his hand traveling up to cup her breast and thumb the tight bud of her nipple. "Ever played with a flogger before?"

"No." She arched her back just a little, pressing her breast into his hand. "But until just now I'd never played with handcuffs, exotic body jewelry or gel that gets hot when you blow on it, either."

"Some women really like the stimulation." Jason rubbed his thumb over her nipple again. "Done just right, it increases circulation. Down here." His hand moved down her body until it

159

just brushed the pubic curls at the apex of her thighs through the thin cotton of her borrowed shirt. "Makes the blood rush to this region, which causes your labia to swell and pulse. Stimulates your nerve endings in a way you can't with hands, each little leather strap fanning out to make contact with the soft skin of your bare ass and the backs of your thighs."

Cass made a gulping noise and felt her knees sag. "Doesn't that hurt?"

"Do you want to find out, Cass?" Jason asked the question as he bunched the fabric of the tee shirt up, exposing her sex. His hand followed the bared curve of her hip up to her waist. Her muscles tightened in reaction to his touch and she felt her belly flutter. "I think you do."

Cass could feel her heart rate and respiration spiraling out of control, her pulse thudding and making an answering pulse beat between her legs. She made an unintelligible sound in response.

"But first, I think we'll have some pizza." He squeezed her waist before releasing his grip and letting the shirt fall back into place to cover her. But he kept his arm around her, holding her. "If we're going to play those kinds of games, I want your full attention. If you're hungry, you'll be distracted."

Cass gave an audible gulp.

Jason laughed, a warm, deep sound, and his hand pressed into her belly. "You're going to like it," he informed her. "You got so excited by the idea. And now you're nervous, and that's exciting, too, isn't it?"

"Maybe," she said, feeling cautious. Her voice came out a little hoarse. She cleared her throat and said, "So. Pizza."

"Pizza." He stroked her from belly to hip, reversing his earlier caress, and then stepped back, releasing her. "Why don't you sit down. I'll take care of this."

"Okay." Since she wasn't sure how much longer her legs were going to last, Cass made her way to a kitchen chair and perched on it, curling one leg under her. She watched as Jason retrieved a cardboard box from the refrigerator, arranged slices on their plates and placed one in the microwave.

It seemed both strange and comfortable to be here in his kitchen. Their kitchen now, she supposed. When she'd gotten on the plane, he'd been a stranger to her. He'd been inside her less than half an hour ago, and he'd graphically described what he planned to do to her body next. Now he was working in the kitchen while she watched him, creating a sense of familiarity at odds with the length of time she'd known him.

Jason set a plate in front of her, handed her a fork, and seated himself opposite her across the little table. He caught her looking at him and asked, "Need anything else?"

Cass gave her head a slow shake. "No," she said. The pizza smelled delicious and made her realize how hungry she was. The man across from her made her feel warm inside and out, and she had a very satisfied kind of ache between her thighs that had already shifted to interest in more. And she'd beaten Riley in spite of his underhanded methods. This was almost a perfect moment, and Cass savored it while she smiled at Jason. "Thank you," she added, remembering her manners.

"My pleasure." His eyes glowed with warmth as they held hers. "And yours."

The sexual reference made her smile widen in agreement, although she felt compelled to point out, "A gentleman doesn't brag."

"A gentleman wouldn't know how to use that bag of toys you're enjoying so much." He grinned at her and forked up a bite of pizza.

"When you can make me feel that good, I guess bragging is

allowed," Cass said as she followed suit, digging in to the impromptu meal. And he had a point. Would a gentleman have handcuffed her and given her mind-shattering oral sex on top of a bar? Would a gentleman have suggested flogging her and then proceeded to describe the sensations it would arouse?

She might not be married to a perfect gentleman, but at least as far as sexual compatibility went, he was the perfect man.

Besides, she wasn't much of a lady herself. She'd let him take her on top of a bar table, come her brains out when he did it, and then told him to give it to her hard from behind when they finally made it to the bedroom. Hardly the picture of restraint.

Which made them pretty well matched.

They ate in comfortable silence. Jason cleared their plates away afterwards and rinsed them before loading them into the dishwasher. He turned to look at her, those warm whiskey eyes of his taking her in. "Ready?"

Cass uncurled herself from her chair and stood. "I'm ready." Sort of. Now that the moment was at hand, she wasn't sure she was up to anything this adventurous.

When she worried her lower lip with her teeth, Jason shook his head at her and held out his hand. "Come here."

"I did it again, didn't I?" Cass asked. She walked to him and put her hand in his. "The lip thing. I didn't even know I was doing it until you caught me."

"Told you." He smiled at her and pulled her closer until their bodies just touched. "You do not have a poker face."

"Good thing I don't play poker."

"Not even strip poker?"

"Um. No." Cass leaned just a little bit closer to him, letting her breasts brush his chest, teasing both of them with the contact. "You'd probably make losing really fun, though."

"We'll have to try it and find out." He brought their joined hands up to his mouth and kissed hers. "If you're having second thoughts about the flogger, it can stay put away."

"I trust you," Cass said. "You knew how to use all the other toys to very good effect. I'm sure you know what to do with the little pink whip. And no, I do not want to hear about how you learned these tricks or how many women you've practiced them on tonight."

"Cass." Jason let go of her hand and wrapped his arms around her, pulling her closer until her body fit tightly against his. "There's never been a woman like you."

"That's good," she said into his bare chest. "Because I've never known a man like you, either." She relaxed into his hold and felt him rub his jaw against the top of her head, a rough caress that made her belly quiver. "Jason."

"Yes?" His voice sounded deep and smooth and it flowed over her as the sound and scent of him made her feel lightheaded.

"I don't think I want to try that tonight." She rubbed her cheek against his chest and breathed him, pressing closer as if she could absorb him into her pores. "It was fun in the bar. The toys made a good ice breaker. And what you described, um. It made me feel—well, I think I want to try that someday. But not right now. Right now I want just us. No toys. No tricks."

"Just us and a bed?" Jason rocked his hips into hers, letting her feel the fullness of his erection.

She nodded.

"You've got it." He turned them both and shifted his hold to tuck her into his side, one arm still holding her close. "The bed's this way."

Cass leaned into him and let him lead her back to his bedroom, feeling a different sort of anticipation building. She knew what he felt like against her, inside her. She knew how perfectly matched they were physically, and how thoroughly he'd satisfy her. She also knew what it was like to cry in his arms, to argue with him, to laugh with him. In less than a day together, it seemed like she'd run through the full spectrum of emotions, and in every mood, they'd meshed.

"I liked you," she said out loud as they walked. "Before we met. I liked the way you put things. I liked your priorities. Sometimes it seemed like I was missing some meaning in what you said, but I liked you. Your emails made me feel good. I was nervous about meeting you because I was a little bit afraid that I'd lose that. That I wouldn't feel connected, or attracted, or it would just be wrong once we met in person."

His arm around her tightened. "You didn't seem overwhelmed by me at first."

"I thought I was meeting somebody else," Cass pointed out. "I was attracted to you and trying not to be. I was annoyed because I didn't want to feel that for the wrong man."

"I was annoyed because you insisted on preferring another man who wasn't even there to me." Jason halted her by the bed and took hold of the hem of her tee shirt, drawing it slowly up her body and over her head. She raised her arms, slipping them free of the sleeves, then started helping him off with his shorts in the spirit of fair play.

"You're the only man here now," Cass said as they worked his shorts off together. She reached out to wrap her hand around the smooth length of his erection. "And you don't feel wrong to me."

"There's only one thing that feels more right than your hand around me," Jason said as her hand glided up and down his shaft. "And if you keep doing that, you're going to find yourself on your back with your legs spread while I experience it."

She grinned at him, following his meaning without any difficulty. "Are you talking about sex?"

"I'm talking about getting inside you." He worked a hand between her thighs, retaliating by stroking her sex while she stroked his. "Deep inside you, as far as I can go, as far as you can take me, your body fitting around me like a hot, tight glove."

Cass stared at him and had to remind herself to keep breathing. She swallowed hard and tried to stay upright. "I think my legs are going to collapse," she informed him. "You can't just say something like that and expect me not to fall onto the nearest horizontal surface."

"There's one right here." Jason smiled at her. "Soft, comfortable, available. Convenient."

"Then why are we standing here talking?" She released him and jumped onto the bed, trusting him to follow her.

He tackled her, grabbing her around the waist, flipping her onto her back and caging her in place with his arms and legs. "Would you prefer lying here talking?"

"I don't know how safe talking is." Cass stared up at him, suddenly feeling an edge of apprehension. What if he said something that made the warm glow of happiness and lust evaporate? "I'm enjoying this too much," she blurted out. "I haven't felt so good in, well, I don't know. Maybe I've never felt this good. Maybe it's too good to be true and it can't last, but if it is, I'm not ready to hear that."

"Cass." His eyes darkened and he lowered his mouth to hers.

Warm, exploring, inviting, his lips moved over hers and

165

coaxed them to soften and open for him. When she did, the kiss deepened until she lost her breath. He raised his head and looked into her eyes as she gazed back at him, trying to make her lungs work.

"How about if we keep to only here and now," Jason suggested. "No yesterday, no tomorrow."

She touched her tongue to her lower lip. "That might work."

He smiled at her. "It works for me. Right here and now, there's just the two of us. Alone. And I want you again."

"Oh." Cass blinked at him, at a loss for anything more to say. He only had to say he wanted her and her body said *yes*. "Good."

"Very."

Jason kissed her again, taking his time about it, a thorough, lazy exploration that finally ended when her heart was pounding and she'd forgotten everything but him. His body settled against hers, his legs prodding hers to separate and make a space for him. Cass put her hands on his shoulders, just touching at first, then let herself explore. He reciprocated, rolling with her onto their sides to make it easier.

She followed the line of his back and the planes and angles his chest and arms made. She caught his reaction when her hand trailed over his abdomen and raised a brow at him. "Ticklish?"

"Yes. And if you take advantage of that, I'll get even."

That opened up too many possibilities to contemplate them all. As long as the handcuffs were within easy reach, she decided she was better off not testing him. "No tickling," Cass agreed.

"Turn over on your belly."

"Why?" She felt her eyes go wider. "I didn't tickle you."

"I'm not going to do anything to you." Jason grinned at her. "At least, nothing you won't like. Turn over."

She gave him a measuring look. "Nothing funny."

"Nothing funny," he promised.

"Okay." Cass turned over and settled herself on her stomach, arms folded to make a pillow for her head. She felt his hand rest on her lower back and sighed at the warm pressure there. He massaged in a slow circle, then made his way up her spine. He smoothed her hair over one shoulder and began to massage her neck, fingers working up around the base of her skull and then back down, digging into the pressure points along her shoulders.

She exhaled and felt tension easing away as her muscles loosened under his skilled manipulation. "That feels wonderful."

"That's the idea."

He kissed her shoulder and began to rub between the blades, easing muscles she hadn't even known were there, smoothing the larger muscles of her back in long strokes. He returned to her lower back, moving back and forth across, each stroke bringing his hand farther down until he settled his palm over the curve of her bare butt.

"Mm," she sighed. "That's nice."

"Nice?" He increased the pressure, moving his hand over her ass, a familiar, intimate, lover's touch that made her sex clench in anticipation.

Move your hand lower, Cass silently directed. She shifted her thighs apart in invitation, but Jason ignored her.

"Jason," she said out loud.

"Yes?" His fingertips teased the insides of her thighs. "Did you want something?"

"You."

"You have me."

Cass gritted her teeth as he toyed with the lower curve of her butt, stroking the soft skin of her thighs but refusing to reach between them. "I'm not going to beg," she said, willing it to be true.

"You won't have to." He kissed the nape of her neck, the curve of her shoulder, his breath sending heat and a frisson of excitement along her skin. "I plan to leave you thoroughly satisfied, Cass."

"Before or after I lose my fragile grip on sanity?"

"You seem pretty sane to me. A little stressed, maybe. Definitely excited. But I don't think your grip on sanity is in any danger."

"You so underestimate yourself." Cass arched her lower back in an unmistakable message. "Extended foreplay from you would be enough to break the mind of a much stronger woman than I am." And right now, she didn't feel strong at all. She felt weak, hot, receptive and almost aching with need.

"You're not going to rush me this time."

He nipped at the sensitive point where neck and shoulder joined, scraping her skin with his teeth until she shuddered. His fingertips stroked in a counter caress, and Cass subsided into the mattress, surrendering to the moment.

"Okay," she agreed. "I won last time."

"You'll win this time, too." Jason teased her earlobe with his teeth. "Slow can be its own reward."

"Or torture."

"You're going to make such a lousy martyr when you come screaming."

Cass laughed out loud at that, then sighed as his hands, the warmth of his body, the brush of his lips and the pace he refused to hasten soothed and heated her at the same time. Her body felt more relaxed than she remembered being since the day she got dumped and fired, and all of her felt alive and aware. Nerve endings hummed as her mind relaxed, too.

When he finally nudged her hip, prodding her to roll onto her side again, Cass complied with a lazy, languorous stretch. Her breasts felt full and heavy and when he settled his hands over them she let out a low moan of pleasure.

"Like that?"

"Mmm." She lifted heavy eyelids halfway to look at him, her lips curving in a warm smile. "Yes."

"What about this?" Jason squeezed and kneaded the soft flesh that filled his hands.

"That, too." Her tongue felt thick, making speech awkward.

When his hands released her, she made a soft sound of regret that turned to another sigh as he stroked the sensitive skin of her belly, her hips, and finally settled one hand over her mound, pressing lightly against her sex.

"Jason." She shifted, opening herself to his touch. "Yes."

"I like hearing you say that." He kissed her again, his mouth warm and firm on hers. "Makes me want to think of creative and interesting ways to make you say it again."

"Your name? Or yes?" Cass asked against his lips.

"I meant yes. But both, now that you mention it." Jason nipped lightly at her lower lip and stroked his hand between her legs at the same time.

Cass gave up on talking. A few minutes later, he stopped tormenting both of them and retrieved another condom. When he slid inside her, she closed her eyes, almost unable to believe how perfectly they fit together, how good and right it felt. It was slower this time, less urgent but no less intense, and Cass gave herself up to the sensations and emotions he aroused.

Her last coherent thought was that tomorrow could take care of itself.

Jason rocked into Cass again and again, with each stroke feeling more a part of her, as if the union of their bodies was creating another, deeper tie. Her eyes were dark with pleasure and emotion, a light flush colored her skin, and her hair spilled around her in a silken tangle. "You look so beautiful," he said, holding her eyes as he moved above and inside her.

"I feel beautiful." She smiled at him, then let her eyes drift shut as her body arched into his. "This feels beautiful."

"It should." Jason claimed her lips in another long, unhurried kiss, savoring the reaction that surged through him like a drug.

She made him feel powerful, victorious and possessive. He wanted to brand her body with his, forge a bond that couldn't be broken easily. She might be his wife, but the tie felt entirely too tenuous for his peace of mind. The knowledge that she could walk away from him, or worse, be hurt by his unintended deception drove him to make her his in the most basic and elemental way.

He drew it out, loving her with slow deliberation, until she was gasping and writhing under him. Then he felt her inner muscles clench around his shaft and lost the battle for control. Passion swept them both away and he spent himself inside her until there was nothing left to give.

Jason noted that even in the aftermath, when she lay spent and limp in his arms, Cass clung to him, holding onto him as if she felt what he felt, the compulsion to hang on to what they'd found and not let go.

His arms were locked around her, and it wasn't until he

realized that she slept in his embrace that he found the will to loosen his hold. He left her just long enough to dispose of the condom and retrieve the clothes they'd left scattered around the bar. When he returned to the bed, she stirred and burrowed into him as if she'd missed the warmth of his body and sought him even in sleep.

For a long time Jason laid awake, holding her close, feeling the silk of her hair and the satin of her skin against his, listening to the rhythm of her heart.

Mine, he thought, and wondered if it would be true in the morning. Whatever happened, he wasn't about to let her go without a fight. No matter how it had started, no matter how many lies lay between them, they'd found something real. Something that deserved time to grow.

Chapter Eleven

Cass woke up to Rex licking her hand and whining at her. She blinked her eyes open, rolled towards the edge of the bed and peered at the large canine. He was doing a very good doggie pantomime of having to go that stopped just short of crossing all four of his paws.

A Rex accident in the bedroom didn't strike her as a very good way to start the day. And God knew the marriage already had enough problems. So Cass slid out of bed and into the jeans she'd worn yesterday, unzipped her suitcase for everything else, dressing as quietly as she could so she didn't wake up Jason. If he ran a bar, he probably worked nights. She hadn't asked, but in the meantime, she could let the man sleep.

Neither of them had gotten much of that last night, but considering how much she'd gotten of something else, Cass wasn't going to complain. A night of great sex was more than a fair trade for a solid night's sleep.

She slung her Nikon around her neck and signaled for Rex to follow her, not that he needed any encouragement. Her head felt light from overindulging in spiked punch and Jason and the sun looked way too bright. Coffee, Cass decided. She'd probably find that in the kitchen. If not, she could go downstairs and brew coffee in the bar. Although she wasn't sure she could look at the bar counter without blushing.

The kitchen did have a coffeemaker, grounds and filters. Cass set it up to brew, then poured some for herself as soon as enough liquid dripped into the pot to fill a cup.

Rex let out another whine.

"Coming," Cass told the dog. She rummaged under the kitchen sink and found a plastic bag for doggie cleanup. She stuffed it into her pocket, clutched her cup in one hand and headed for the stairs. Rex led the way. She grabbed his leash and attached it to his collar while he quivered with urgency, then took him outside to find a good spot to take care of business.

Half an hour later, Cass had finished her coffee, snapped a few images of Ketchikan, and walked Rex long enough for both of them to feel ready for the day.

She started turning over the previous day's events in her mind. As the reality of it all sunk in she realized she'd need to fax a copy of the marriage certificate to her attorney's office right away. He'd need proof that she'd fulfilled the terms by the deadline. She'd also need to call Lisa and give her The Last Resort's phone number. The mental checklist of business to take care of calmed her.

No matter what happened with Jason, no matter what unpleasant revelations he had for her today, he'd helped her secure her inheritance and thwart Riley. Cass wasn't sure which of those things gave her more satisfaction, but either way, she was grateful to him for marrying her. He'd had his reasons for the haste and deception, she supposed. She'd certainly had hers. And now, well, she'd just see.

This line of thinking made her nervous so she focused on the next step. The next step was to find the paperwork, locate a fax machine, and get the legalities established. Jason's bar probably had a fax machine, and the paperwork was there, too.

It was easier to think about that than to wonder what surprises were in store for her today, especially when Jason had seemed so sure they weren't the good kind. Thinking about that made her stomach lurch and her chest tighten.

Yesterday might have been the most bizarre day of her life, but it had certainly ended on an all-time high. The memory of Jason snapping the handcuffs on her was going to remain sharp and clear in her head when she was ninety.

Think about that, Cass, she lectured herself. Erotic scenes replaying in her brain might make it hard to carry out the fax mission, but it'd make a much more pleasant distraction than worrying about the unknown.

Something just ahead caught her eye, and Cass automatically lifted the camera, zoomed in and framed her shot before what she was looking at registered. When it did, she lowered the camera and stared at the sign that looked like a sideways ruler with a cheerful figure of a fisherman on top and the words Liquid Sunshine Gauge spelled out in sunny yellow.

She'd already discovered one thing Jason hadn't wanted her to know.

When Jason woke up to an empty bed, he came all the way awake in a hurry. A missing wife struck him as a very bad sign and added a certain level of urgency to the morning. Who knew what she was doing while he slumbered ignorantly on? Who knew what Sam or somebody else would tell her without checking to see how much she knew first? Jason didn't know, but he could imagine a list of potentially explosive discoveries that had him catapulting through dressing and out the bedroom door in search of her.

He found her in the kitchen, seated in a chair with the creature she passed off to the world as a dog collapsed in a panting heap at her feet and a cup of coffee in her hands.

"Good morning," Jason said, trying to see enough of her face to gauge her mood. Her head swung up, but her closed expression gave nothing away. That in itself was bad. "Been up long?"

"Long enough." She looked back down at her cup. "Rex needed a walk."

Long enough for what? Coffee and grounds for divorce? "Is there more of that?" Jason asked. If the whole truth was going to come out, he wanted his brain sharp and clear for the event.

Cass waved wordlessly towards the coffeepot. Jason poured a cup and took a seat opposite her. He didn't have to wait long for her to fill the silence.

"When were you going to tell me?" Her eyes locked onto his and he tried to guess how much she knew.

"About?" Jason sent the verbal volley back into her court.

"It does rain in Ketchikan, you know," Cass mimicked his words from the previous night and Jason felt the tension in his gut relax. So that's what she'd discovered. She went on, "In fact, it rains a lot. A hundred and sixty-two inches is a lot, wouldn't you say?"

"It's a fair amount," Jason agreed.

"It's a deluge," Cass said. "Calling it liquid sunshine does not change thirteen and a half feet of rain a year into a bright forecast." She took another swallow and set her cup down. "It rains so much, in fact, that the local saying goes if you can't see Deer Mountain, it's raining. And if you can see it, it's about to rain. That's what you stopped Sam from saying in the airport." She gave him an accusing look.

Jason was only too happy to agree. "That's right," he said, trying to project sincerity and regret. "I didn't want you to judge our future based on weather."

"What should I judge it on? Sex?"

Oh, if only it could be so simple. "It's a thought. Chemistry and physical compatibility are location independent. And it's an important part of a long-term relationship. If you didn't think so, why did you feel it was important to meet me in person before you'd marry me?"

She tilted her head and considered him. "Well, I admit, that was an important part of it. If I couldn't imagine myself responding to you physically, I didn't think we'd have a chance at making it work long term."

"If last night wasn't enough of a test run for you, there are still some toys in that bag we haven't played with." Jason did his best to sound helpful and accommodating. "I don't think you should rush to judge our sex life without trying out all the variations first."

Cass gave him a speculative look. "I'm not sure a single night is enough to base any conclusions on."

"Did I mention the advantage of very long nights during part of the year?" Jason leaned forward and touched her hand. She turned it palm up to clasp his.

"You did, yes." A smile played around the corners of her mouth. "Long nights without a partner probably get pretty lonely. Long nights with the wrong partner might be even worse."

The thought of long nights with Cass rose in Jason's mind like a mirage. Her long legs wrapped around him, her hair spilling across the sheets, his body driving endlessly into hers. "Long nights with the right partner might not seem long enough."

Desire edged his voice and he saw the answering awareness in her eyes. Her hand clutched his and the air between them grew as charged with tension as the electric buildup before a storm.

Her lips parted, and her lids lowered partway. "Jason." His name came out in a whisper of sound, but he heard her as clearly as if she'd shouted.

"Come over here." He wanted to drag her across the table and into his lap, but he forced himself to wait while she got to her feet to accept his growled invitation. Triumph shot through him as she came to him, proof that their physical connection at least ran both ways.

"Jason." Cass said his name again, and he stood up to meet her.

"I like it when you say my name." He settled his hands on her hips and pulled her closer, until her body nestled into his. "I especially like the way you say it when I'm inside you."

"I like the way it feels when you're inside me," she said. Her hands moved up his arms and rested on his shoulders.

"Something we have in common." Jason's hands tightened on her hips as he rocked his pelvis into hers. "You might like it enough to overlook a little rain."

Cass laughed and rubbed her cheek against his chest. "It's not a little rain. I bet everybody in town has an ark waiting in their backyard."

"Our bedroom is upstairs," he said, smiling at her answer. "That should make you feel safer if the threat of rising water makes you nervous."

"As long as the roof doesn't leak, we'll probably be okay."

If the roof leaked, he probably wouldn't notice. Cass naked in bed with him could make him oblivious to anything short of the four horsemen of the Apocalypse riding through their room.

"We'll have the roof inspected," Jason promised. "In the

meantime, I think we need to inspect the mattress. Did it sound squeaky to you last night?"

"I think the squeaky noises all came from me." She pressed into him and he felt the heat of her through the layers of clothes that separated them.

"Along with a few moans and sighs and gasps." Jason kept her body tight against his as he walked her backwards. "I still think we ought to make sure the bed's sound."

"Um." Cass moved with him and let him maneuver her into the bedroom until the backs of her legs met the edge of the bed.

He lowered her onto it and started undressing her with more haste than finesse. She didn't seem to mind. Her eyes had darkened to midnight blue and her breasts rose and fell as her breath came faster. "You're taking too long."

"You don't want me to hurry too much." Jason grinned down at her and peeled her shirt up, exposing her midriff and the curves of her breasts spilling out of her bra. His lips explored the skin his hands bared while he pulled the shirt over her head and tossed it aside, then unhooked her bra and stripped that away, too.

He drew one nipple into his mouth, listened to her sigh of pleasure, and went to work on her jeans. She helped him, raising her hips while he shimmied her pants down. He had to stop his oral exploration long enough to step back and get the jeans off her legs, followed by her underwear, leaving her sprawled naked on the bed.

"Nice." Jason filled his eyes with the sight of her while he got rid of his own clothes.

She gave him a half smile. "I don't feel nice at all right now."

"Naughty is nice in its own way." He brought his mouth down to kiss the soft skin of her belly before working lower and

178

she slipped away, evading him.

"No. My turn."

"We can do it together," Jason suggested.

Cass shook her head, sending her long hair sliding over her breasts in a very distracting way. "I won't be able to concentrate."

That made his cock turn even harder. The thought of her soft lips on him, giving him her full attention, all of her concentration centered on his shaft filling her mouth made him want to spill down her throat.

"I'm not sure this is a good idea," he said as he joined her on the bed.

"I am." She gave him a wicked smile and slid down him, the silk curtain of her hair slipping over his skin before her lips found the head of his cock.

Her tongue danced around his crown, teasing and tasting him, and then she wrapped her mouth around him and brought as much of him inside as she could take.

"God." He fisted his hands in her hair and tried to keep still, to let her set the pace and control the depth of penetration she could comfortably accept. "I hope you don't plan to keep that up very long, because I won't last five minutes if you do."

She licked her way up his shaft, let his head slide free of her mouth, and laughed, a low, throaty sound. "Now you know how it feels to be on the receiving end."

"Let me show you how it feels." Jason urged her upwards with his hands, felt her head shake in response.

"No. I'm in charge this time." She kissed her way down to his balls and Jason sucked in a breath when she very carefully drew one into her mouth.

"Stop that. Right now."

"Why? You don't like it?" She released him and raised her head to ask the question.

"I love it. I'm going to come instantly if you do that again." He reached for her shoulders and tugged upwards again. This time she came with him, fitting her body over his.

The softness of her breasts against his bare chest and the press of her sex against the head of his cock made him want to hold her hips in place while he thrust home, but she wanted to lead this time and he was going to let her. As long as she didn't kill them both in the process.

"Can't have that," Cass sighed, nuzzling his neck. "I want you inside me when you come."

"Then take me inside you."

She rocked her pelvis into his, sliding the heat of her sex along the length of his, until his head pressed against her slick opening. Her flesh gave easily for his, soft and ready, willing. Then she moved away. "Condoms."

"Over there." Jason pointed, admired the view as she bent and stretched to reach, and then he didn't have any words as she tore the packet open and sheathed him, her fingers stroking his shaft in the process.

Cass rose over him, her thighs open, knees resting on either side of his hips, her naked breasts a feast for his eyes. Then she lowered herself onto him and he thrust up to meet her, filling her, giving himself.

"Jason." Her eyes were so dark they looked like a midnight sky. She collapsed forward onto his chest, and then neither of them said anything as their bodies rocked together, faster and faster, overtaken by need and urgency.

He groaned her name when he felt her flesh rippling around his shaft as her orgasm began, gripping and releasing and gripping him again, her pleasure triggering his as he spilled himself in a rush of heat.

A long time later, Cass stirred on top of him. "I should move."

"Why?" Jason stroked her hair and explored the line of her back with lazy fingers.

"Well, for starters, the condom could come off."

"That would be bad," Jason said, although the risk of pregnancy didn't sound all that dreadful to him. Just the opposite. He made no move to withdraw from the clasp of her flesh.

"Uh huh." Cass agreed, but he noticed she didn't move, either.

"Unless you didn't mind." He smoothed her hair back and let his fingers work in towards her scalp, lightly massaging. "You did say you wanted a family."

"I do." She rubbed her cheek against his shoulder. "But now is probably a bad time to get pregnant, since there's a whole lot you haven't told me yet."

"There is that." Jason turned on his side, taking her with him, sliding out of her in the process. "Stay here. I'll be back."

Cass watched him walk away through half-lidded eyes, then rolled onto her stomach and blew out a long breath. There might still be things she didn't know, but she did know something. She knew Jason made her nerve endings sizzle, made heat coil inside her, and that physically at least the two of them fit together like two halves of a whole.

She also knew he'd done more than her previous fiancés had done. He'd shown up for the wedding. In fact, he'd pretty much conned her into the ceremony and hustled her down the aisle before she could back out, with his friends surrounding her, aiding and abetting him.

That told her something else. Jason had loyal friends, people who cared about him, spoke well of him. A man's friends revealed a lot about the man. She thought of Mona's gift bag and muffled a laugh. At least his friends weren't stuffy.

He ran a business. She knew how much time, energy and dedication that took. He'd been doing it for two years. That demonstrated the ability to stick with a commitment.

He'd teased her, talked to her, comforted her, danced with her. He'd shown her insight, tenderness, possessiveness and a heated lust that stole her breath. Being with Jason made her feel even better than reading his words on a computer screen.

There was still something she was missing, a subtext that she couldn't read. But the sex between them was as raw and honest as it was explosive. He wasn't holding anything back or hiding anything from her in bed. He wanted her. Whatever else might be going on, that was real.

And she wanted him. All of him, with no more secrets between them.

Which meant she needed to reveal one of her own.

If they were going to really talk, she'd better get dressed. Tempting as it might be to stay in bed and try to avoid it for a while longer, it was probably better to get it over with now. Down the hall, she heard the shower come on and knew it'd be a few minutes before Jason returned. Cass sat up, already feeling chilled without his warmth beside her, and retrieved the clothes he'd stripped off her and scattered.

She'd just finished dressing when the phone started to ring down in the bar. It might be bar business, or it might be Lisa returning her call. Since Jason wouldn't hear the phone over the sound of running water, she ran downstairs and picked up the phone on the fifth ring.

"Last Resort," she said, her voice sounding unnaturally chipper to her own ears for this hour of the day. That's what a night of including barred great sex could do, make even the darkest morning seem bright. Of course, going back to bed for a follow-up bout of morning-after sex didn't hurt, either.

"Cass?"

"Lisa!" The sound of her friend's voice made Cass smile. "I'm so glad you called back. What happened with the audition?"

"First tell me what happened with Bluebeard."

"He doesn't have a beard," Cass said.

Lisa made a rude sound. "I'm not interested in his facial hair or lack of. I want juicy details."

"I'm married," Cass announced, figuring that was pretty juicy. Then she frowned and added, "I think. It was kind of surreal and I'm not sure it was legal. But I faxed the paperwork to my attorney's office before I called you this morning."

"This sounds interesting. I'm going to get comfortable."

"Well, let me know when you're sitting down."

"I'm sitting now. And you should have asked that before you told me you got married without me. In a hurry, was he?"

"No, I had to tell him to hurry up," Cass said, distracted by the memory. "Oh. Sorry. Too much information."

Lisa's laughter rang out. "Bluebeard has some good stuff in his closet?"

Cass thought about the bag of toys. "You have no idea," she said with feeling.

"Well, he didn't look like the type, but I'm glad you're having fun with him. Now tell me about the possibly not legal wedding."

"He does look the type. The picture wasn't him," Cass said.

183

"It's a long story. Actually, I'm still waiting to hear the story. We got sidetracked when he was about to tell all." She grinned, thinking that Mona's bag of tricks would have derailed that conversation even if Jason hadn't already suggested they postpone the day of reckoning.

"Fascinating," Lisa said in her best Spock voice. "So he sent you a phony photo, hustled you into a phony wedding, and then I'm guessing you got something that wasn't fake."

"Very real," Cass assured her. The Bad Boy vibrator could stay in the bag. "But enough about my new sex life. Tell me about you."

"I got it," Lisa said. "And there's more. Are you sitting down?"

Cass hitched her hip onto a barstool. "Close enough. Go ahead."

"I'm The Sirens' new drummer. We went straight into working out schedules, they gave me material, the works. There's a new album coming up and we're pretty much going straight into the studio. And Lorelei doesn't want the photographer that did the last cover shoot. They were talking about who they could get and I told them you were good, listed some of your credits. Lorelei wanted to see some examples."

Lisa paused to take a breath and Cass shifted to put her whole weight onto the barstool. Her legs had gone weak. "You want me to send some portfolio shots?" she asked.

"No, I had the prints of those art shots you're always taking of me. You know, the ones where the colors look fake?"

"Cross-processing," Cass said automatically.

"And the ones that are sort of like black and white but not."

"Infrared."

"Yeah, those. Well, I showed them to the band and they

went nuts for them. Lorelei wants you on the shoot. Can you come back to Seattle?"

All the air had left her lungs. *Breathe,* Cass told herself. She inhaled and then exhaled a couple of times.

"Still there?" Lisa asked. "Is it too short notice? They want you right away. Today. So there's time to work with the designers and all the other stuff that has to be coordinated for the photo shoot. Oh, and your travel expenses are covered up front. Say when and I'll get your plane ticket reserved." She paused. "I want you here. Please say you'll take the job."

Cass let out a shaky laugh. "I'm not insane enough to turn down an opportunity like this. I'll take the job, I think. Tell me a little about them, are they good to work with? Did you click with them? No, forget I asked. Of course you clicked, if you didn't, you wouldn't have joined the band."

"Cass. You're babbling."

"You'd babble, too," Cass said. "You probably did already. You got it out of your system before you called me."

"Guilty," Lisa said. "I also didn't sleep at all and I'm so wired on caffeine I'm practically vibrating. But in spite of this, I know you will make me look amazing on film so I won't cringe if I see myself on a billboard."

"You already look amazing."

"Maybe, but you can make me look that way in a photo, and that's why the band loved the pictures. Some people can make even beautiful women look awful. You can make average people look beautiful. And your pictures look sort of daydreamy, which is even better. We're supposed to look like legends, that's the album theme."

"Legends," said Cass. She could picture it in her mind, a series of portraits of legendary women looking larger than life and yet unmistakably human in their emotions. "Yes. Okay. I'll be there. I need to figure out ferry schedules and available flight times, but yes. I want the job."

She hung up in a daze. Her feet found their way up the stairs as the shower shut off. She went to the kitchen, dumped out the cup of coffee she'd abandoned when Jason had offered her something hotter, and refilled the mug.

She heard Jason's footsteps in the hall. "Cass?"

Oh, right. He'd expected to find her in the bedroom. "In here."

He filled the doorframe a moment later, his hair still wet from the shower, his whiskey eyes drinking her up. "There you are."

She nodded. The air felt tense and not with the electric rush of sex. This was it. He was going to tell her the thing she didn't really want to know but had to hear if they were going to go forward.

"Cass." He rubbed a hand over his face, then shoved both hands into his pockets as if he didn't trust himself not to reach for her. "About the photo and the fake name. I lied in the ad. I wasn't looking for a wife."

"Oh," Cass said. There didn't seem to be any other words. She hadn't known what to expect, but whatever explanation she'd imagined was behind his deception, this wasn't it. "What were you looking for?"

"I was looking for a con artist."

That made so little sense that she struggled with it for a few seconds in silence. Then she shook her head. "I'm sorry. What?"

"Miss Lonely Hearts. I was looking for a woman running the Miss Lonely Hearts con game, and she seemed to have targeted The Last Resort. I went after her when I found out she'd hit Sam and the Lawrence brothers."

Chapter Twelve

Con artist? Cass replayed Jason's words in her head as if that would help her understand. Sam she remembered with no trouble. The Lawrence brothers took another beat to place. "The twins? Those two big men who could be poster children for the strong, silent type?"

Jason nodded. "I used the fake name and another man's photo in case it was somebody who knew me, who knew the regulars at the bar, and had some kind of agenda. I posted my ad as bait, and you were the one I hooked. It was an honest mistake. You matched the description, and she'd given her location as Seattle. I showed your picture to Sam, Dwight and Duke and none of them told me I had the wrong woman."

"Oh," Cass said again as the words sank in. He hadn't been looking for love, he'd been looking for justice. Or revenge. But not for her. She was here with him only because he'd made a mistake.

"Please say something else." His eyes bored into hers, his usual easy smile nowhere in sight.

She said the first thing that came to her. "You didn't want a wife." He didn't want her. Same song, third verse. What was wrong with her?

"I wanted you."

That she believed. At least, she believed he wanted her for

now. The chemistry between them was something Jason couldn't possibly have predicted. But wanting each other's bodies wasn't enough. Was it? Before she'd met Jason she wouldn't have said so. Now she didn't know and it was all too much to process. "Was the wedding legal?"

"Yes."

His answer left her no less confused or off-balance, but Cass felt something relax inside her. One major problem at least had been resolved, her inheritance was secure. That was one goal achieved. With Lisa's phone call, another was within reach. The Sirens shoot could launch her photography career into the stratosphere. And that left the last and most important item to her, her longing for a family, for love.

Was that within reach, too? Or was she letting mind-bending sex confuse her judgment? She couldn't think, and standing next to the source of her confusion wasn't helping.

"Okay," she said, feeling numb. She set her cup down on the counter. "I have to go."

"Go?" Jason took a step towards her, then checked himself. "All right. I guess I can understand if you need to take a breather for a minute."

"No, I mean I have to go. Back to Seattle," Cass elaborated.

"Cass, don't walk away from me."

"I have to go," she repeated. She started towards the door and stopped just short of his reach. She didn't want to brush past him, didn't want her body to touch his, because she was pretty sure if that happened she'd lose her perspective, followed by her clothes, and until she'd had a chance to think things through, that was a bad idea. "Please move."

His jaw flexed, but he didn't say anything. He moved aside and she edged past him, then made her way to the bedroom. She ran through what she needed for a quick trip and realized all she really had to take was her purse and her camera bag.

What to do about her dog? She wavered for a minute, debating with herself.

It would be ridiculous, not to mention cruel, to drag Rex on another trip before he'd recovered from the trauma of the last one. Leaving Rex behind would also send a clear message to Jason that she was coming back if he had any doubts about that. And if he was even half the man she felt certain he was, her dog would be in good hands while she was gone.

And from a practical perspective, if she couldn't trust him to take care of a dog, how could she ever trust him with a baby? *Show me you're who I think you are, Cass* thought.

If he wasn't, well, better she found out sooner than later. Especially since she now knew she couldn't even stay on the same island he was on and not end up in bed with him. No matter how careful they were, condoms weren't one hundred percent effective. No birth control method was.

She grabbed up the items she needed, slipped down the stairs, and found Rex asleep in the bar. Cass bent to rub his ears. "I have to go now, but I'll be back. Stay with Jason," she told him. "Be good."

He might look ferocious, but she knew Rex would only pose a potential hazard to the floor. And that would only happen if Jason was too slow to take him outside. He'd behave, and she didn't have any real doubt that her dog would be in good hands.

It occurred to her that Jason had had her helpless and handcuffed, and he'd used that position of control to make her crazed with lust. Then he'd thoroughly satisfied her every desire. She'd trusted him with her body and he'd proved himself worthy of that trust.

Could she trust him with her heart? That was the big question.

The next question was, did she still have a choice?

Cass walked out the door, her stomach in knots and her mind in turmoil, and a sinking sense that for better or worse, her heart was already lost. She just hoped the ferry ride and flight would give her enough time to think and enough distance from the situation to decide how she felt about the man who was her husband, and what she wanted to do about their marriage.

It was well into the evening two days later when Cass opened the door to The Last Resort and walked back inside.

She'd had time to think during the trip, which was good, because once she'd arrived in Seattle the shoot had demanded all her energy and concentration. And the first thing she'd realized was that Jason had nothing in common with her two ex-fiancés. Just the opposite. They'd made promises they hadn't kept, while Jason had found himself faced with a woman he hadn't expected to take him up on his proposal and he'd stood by his word.

Maybe he hadn't started out wanting a wife, but it had to mean something that he'd gone through with the wedding. He could have simply explained the situation to her in the airport, apologized for the unintentional deception, and gone on with his life.

But he hadn't. And Cass didn't believe for a minute that he'd gone through with their farce of a wedding just to get the wedding night. If he'd wanted to get her in bed, the electric current arcing between them would have persuaded her without any lies or charades needed.

Why hadn't he come clean first? Maybe because he'd felt

what she'd felt through their email exchanges. Whatever the truth was, she was ready for it now. She squared her shoulders and looked around the bar, letting her eyes adjust to the interior lighting.

There was Jason behind the bar, looking calm and competent, managing to be everywhere he needed to be without any rush or wasted movements. She'd missed the sight of him, missed the sound of his voice, missed the heat of his body and his touch. Cass just stood there for a minute, looking at him and feeling the tightness inside her throat and chest ease.

She watched as he shook his head at one of the Lawrence twins, who was about to feed some salted nuts to a begging Rex. Jason pushed a jar across the bar instead and she grinned when she realized it was full of dog biscuits. It seemed the bar had a new regular.

Sam sat near them, his posture relaxed, moving his hands as he spoke and the silent Lawrence brothers listened.

Standing apart from them, Cass could see the connections between them all. The regulars at The Last Resort were a family of sorts. No wonder Jason had acted on their behalf. No wonder they'd helped him put a surprise wedding together in record time. Had they kept him in the dark about her mistaken identity because they didn't think it was a mistake on his part, after all? She thought so.

She could belong here, too. Be a part of this family. Cass swallowed past the lump in her throat and blinked against a stinging sensation in her eyes. How long had it been since she'd had that? She'd lost her parents, then her grandfather. The family members she'd had left hadn't exactly made up for the loss. Had exacerbated it, in fact.

This tight-knit group of people might be an unorthodox sort of clan, but the way they worked for and against each other showed her they were family by choice, doing what they thought best for each other.

She forced herself to stop looking at Jason and his group of conspirators and start looking for the loose piece in the familial puzzle. There. Cass moved forward and stopped when she reached the table that held a lone and very colorful woman.

"Can I join you, Mona?"

"Oh, honey, of course." Mona smiled at her and waved at an empty seat. "Good thing you're back. If you'd stayed away another night, Jason would've put me behind the bar and gone after you."

"I did call him every day while I was gone," Cass said. Their phone conversations had been brief, but she'd wanted to make sure he understood she hadn't just left, that she'd been offered an opportunity she had to act on. And that she needed to think, which she couldn't seem to do very well with him anywhere in her vicinity.

Professionally, he'd been pleased for her. Personally, her absence had displeased him. Mostly because of the timing and the way things had been left unresolved between them. His manner on the phone had been watchful, for lack of a better word. Which didn't sound right, since he could only hear her. But Cass had had the impression that he was being careful, biding his time, not pushing her to say or do what he wanted but watching for any opening she might give him.

And probably he'd guessed that sleeping alone after sleeping together didn't suit her any better than it suited him. Smart man, letting time and her body's needs work for him and wear her down without him having to do a thing.

Mona shook her head. "A phone call's not much comfort when a man's sleeping alone and doesn't want to be."

It hadn't been much comfort to her, either, Cass thought.

She'd nearly instigated a session of phone sex the previous night and had had to hang up fast before the impulse overcame her.

"Well, I'm back," she said. "And I wanted to thank you for everything you did for our wedding."

Mona looked surprised and touched. "Oh, I didn't do much."

"Actually, you did. If it wasn't for you, Jason and I never would have met, let alone gotten married." She leaned forward and went on, "You see, Jason was looking for a woman in the classifieds, but not for himself."

She watched as the woman's color drained and mute panic appeared in Mona's eyes. "Oh, no."

"Oh, yes." Cass tipped her head and considered the other woman. "You're Miss Lonely Hearts. But you're not a con artist. So why'd you do it?"

Mona's lips trembled. She pressed them together and then took a steadying gulp from her glass before setting it back down with the liquid level considerably reduced. "It was an accident."

Cass tried not to laugh. It took real effort. Mona's face was so tragic that she forced it down, however. "How do you accidentally get engaged to three men?"

Mona's eyes shot over to the group of men seated at the bar and a liquid sheen covered them before she blinked it away.

And Cass saw it then. The last puzzle piece turned and fell into place. "You got emotionally involved. With all of them?"

Mona nodded. "It started because I knew Duke had put an ad online and I thought he needed a little encouragement. Something to build his confidence. I used a false name and picture so he wouldn't suspect it was me. And then Dwight posted an ad, which I should have expected because those

Lawrence twins never do anything they don't do together. So I encouraged him, too. As a friend at first, and then, well, things got complicated. Then Sam—well."

She broke off and twisted her hands together on the table. "I didn't know how to explain, how to choose between them, or how to back out, so I ended it with all of them. Badly. So it would be over and stay over."

"But it's not over. Is it?" Cass waited for the music to pause between songs, for the background noise in the bar to drop a notch. Then she spoke into the lull with her voice pitched to carry. "Why didn't you just tell them all how you felt about them instead of playing Miss Lonely Hearts?"

Four masculine heads swung their way. Three sets of feet came into contact with the floor. Sam and the Lawrence twins exchanged looks. Then all three of them turned the look on Mona.

Cass slid off her seat and moved away, clearing the path for true love to sort itself out. She got a glimpse of Mona's face just before her trio of jilted lovers surrounded her. She looked like a woman presented with the awful dilemma of being forced to choose between milk chocolate, white chocolate or dark when she wanted desperately to devour the whole sampler.

She took Sam's now-vacant seat at the bar and smiled at her husband. "Hi, honey. I'm home."

His lips twitched in response to her humor but his eyes stayed serious. "How did you know?"

"That I'm home? Or who Miss Lonely Hearts was?"

Jason leaned forward at her words. "Tell me about Mona first. Save the best for last."

Cass nodded. "I thought about it, and I realized you were right. It had to be somebody who knew the bar, knew the regulars. But who and why? I guessed Mona, partly because of
194

something she said when she was helping me get ready for the wedding. But I wasn't sure why, until I saw the way she looked at them."

"How did she look at them?"

Cass took a deep breath. "The way I look at you," she said simply.

Jason came around the end of the bar and stood beside her. "Is it anything like the way I look at you?"

"Yes." Cass stood and then she was in his arms, where she'd wanted to be for the last two days and where she wanted to be every day for the rest of their lives. "That's how I know I'm home. Home is where the heart is."

"Cass." Jason's mouth came down on hers and she answered his kiss with all the pent-up feeling that had been building inside her during the hours of her absence.

When Jason finally relinquished his claim on her lips, she leaned into him for support, feeling breathless and dizzy and flushed with heat. "I think it's time for last call," he said.

Cass looked around. "I think the last round was it," she said. "Everybody left." Except Rex, now flopped at their feet in doggie contentment, gnawing on a rawhide chew.

She wondered if Mona had gone home alone or with company, and how the men intended to persuade her to choose. She thought of the bag of toys Jason had spilled onto the bar and started to laugh.

"Wonder if Mona has another one of those little whips? I'd hate to see what would happen if the three of them cornered her with one of those."

Jason laughed, a low rumble she heard in his chest. "Maybe we should make sure ours is accounted for."

"And the handcuffs, too," Cass said, smiling as she thought

about putting them to good use.

"Considering how well-stocked with surprises Mona seems to be, maybe putting them all together isn't a good idea."

"Mona can handle herself. And besides, the four of them put *us* together, directly and indirectly. I figured one good turn deserved another." Cass gave Jason a wicked look. "Enough about them. We really should check on those handcuffs. Lock up. I'll meet you upstairs."

"I'm not sure I want to let you out of my sight just yet." He framed her face with his hands, his eyes meeting hers with an intent look that made her heart flip. "It was a pretty bad moment for me when I came clean with you only to hear you say you were leaving."

"I know." She ran her hands up the front of his shirt, feeling the warmth of him through the fabric. "I'm sorry. It was just sort of too much. All I could think of was that I'd found another man who didn't want to marry me and how could I have made the same damn mistake?"

She paused to breathe, something she seemed to have to remind herself to do often around Jason. Standing so close to him, the two of them touching, it was easy to forget anything else.

Cass forced herself to focus and went on, "But I didn't. I went to find a man through the classifieds because I didn't want to repeat my mistakes, and it actually worked. I might have made mistakes this time, too, but at least they're all new ones."

"I guess I can be glad I have novelty value." Jason kissed her again, a soft, sure brush of his mouth over hers. "But nothing about this feels like a mistake to me."

"Mmm," she sighed in agreement. "Nothing has ever felt more right."

"Guess I should lock the door before somebody else comes

in."

"Good plan." Cass released her hold on him and braced for the wrench of separation as they moved apart. They were like two magnets drawn together, and it took an effort to go against the pull. She reached down to pet Rex, who made happy doggie noises, thumped his tail and wiggled in bliss. "You've made a lot of new friends, haven't you? Bet you didn't miss me at all. You had everybody here spoiling you rotten."

"I gave him one of your shirts to sleep with," Jason said as he flipped the sign on the door from Open to Closed. "And since your scent was here, too, he was pretty calm while you were away." He settled his hands on her shoulders. "Thank you for leaving him. I knew you needed space to think, but that showed a lot of trust and told me you'd be back pretty quickly."

"You didn't think I'd just foisted an ugly dog off on you and run away?"

"You love that dog." Jason stared down at Rex. "I'm glad you had him neutered, though. The canine gene pool couldn't handle the confusion."

"Rex has his own charm," Cass said. "He grows on people."

"Like moss."

Cass laughed and then his arms were around her and the laughter died away. "Upstairs," she said, her voice catching in her throat. "If we start getting naked down here, somebody could come along and catch us in the act." Not that she really thought there'd be any confusion over why he'd closed early. Everybody in town would know what they were doing.

"I like that the minute I touch you, you start thinking naked thoughts."

Naked thoughts. Carnal thoughts. Abandoned, reckless, very far from practical thoughts. They filled her mind and sent her pulse racing, sent fire coursing through her veins and made her sex clench with want. "Upstairs," she managed to repeat. "And we'd better make it fast."

Jason gave a low chuckle, his whiskey-smooth voice rich with masculine satisfaction. "You want me bad."

"Lucky for me, you already are," Cass said, and headed for the stairs before her knees got too weak to make the trip.

"Lucky for you, I'm not afraid to gamble when I think something's worth the risk." Jason stayed right behind her and they made it to the bedroom in what had to be record time.

"I'm not much of a risk." Cass turned to grin at him as she started stripping away her shirt and bra, feeling the rush of cool air on her bare skin. Her nipples tightened in reaction. "I'm a very sure thing."

"It didn't look all that sure at the airport. I thought I was going to lose you before I ever had you." He unbuttoned his shirt, shrugged it off his shoulders and let it drop to the floor. Then his hands went to the snap on his jeans. "I'll see your shirt and raise you pants."

Cass laughed and dropped hers, watching as he unzipped and revealed an impressive erection. "Now what?"

"Now you take off those panties or I tear them in half." Jason bared his teeth at her in a wolfish smile as he finished discarding his jockeys, then stood there hard and male and gloriously naked.

She lost her panties so fast she nearly risked ripping them herself. Cass kicked them away and launched herself at him, sending them both onto the bed in a tangle of limbs. "Where are those handcuffs?" She asked the question in a throaty murmur as her hands ran over his body, touching, exploring, rediscovering.

"Bedside table drawer. Along with the rest of Mona's bag of tricks."

"Mmm. Good." Cass rolled in the indicated direction, fumbled in the drawer and retrieved the cuffs. "Put your hands over your head."

"You want to put them on me?"

"Yes. I'm a firm believer in marital equality."

Jason arched a brow at her, then laid back and stretched his arms up, bringing his wrists together just above his head. The pose displayed his upper body to perfection and Cass got distracted for a minute admiring the view. Then she straddled him and reached up to secure his hands with the cuffs, checking to make sure she could work the catch to release them first.

"Gotcha," she murmured as they snapped closed.

"You pretty much had me at hello," Jason said, misquoting the movie line. "If you wanted to take up the Miss Lonely Hearts con, you'd make a fortune in no time."

"Lucky for us, I don't need to. We already have a fortune." Cass sat back and smiled at him.

His face turned serious. "Cass, I have enough of a cushion saved to be comfortable, and I own this place free and clear, but it's not exactly a fortune."

"I'm not talking about your net worth," she said. "There's something I didn't tell you." She bit her lower lip, feeling nervous now that the moment was at hand. Would he think she'd married him for the money? Well, if he did, she had the upper hand and he was in handcuffs. That should give her a chance to convince him that she wanted him and money had nothing to do with it.

Figuring it was like ripping off a Band-Aid and the best way to handle it was to just get it over with, Cass blurted out, "I'm an heiress."

"You are?" Jason considered her for a long minute. "Well, then, I guess you won't be upset about how much you're going to spend on film and processing, because while you were gone I bought you a Holga."

"You did?" Cass felt a smile spread over her face and warmth spread through her chest.

"Yes. I thought I owed you a wedding present."

"Jason." She lowered herself so that her torso lay on top of his, her knees resting on either side of his hips, their bodies pressed together but not yet joined. "Thank you."

"Feel free to express your gratitude any way that feels right to you." He rocked his pelvis up in a blatant invitation she intended to take him up on. As soon as she finished telling him the rest of it.

"There's more," Cass said. "I had to get married by my twenty-eighth birthday or all the money would go to my remaining relatives. With three million dollars worth of motivation, they did an amazingly good job of making sure I never made it to the altar."

"That would explain why you were willing to let me rush you into saying I do," Jason said. His tone was so even she couldn't read it. Cass raised herself up to look into his face.

"No, I think hormones did that," she admitted. "I saw you, and all my brilliant plans went up in flames. My God, I kissed you. I thought I'd made a commitment to somebody else, a man I felt a strong connection to, and there I was acting like a teenager who didn't know how to handle physical attraction. I thought I'd become the lowest kind of person, a cheater."

"Thank you. I think." His face was as expressionless as his voice and a cold sense of unease crept into her.

"I didn't just get married for the money," Cass said. "Money had nothing to do with the way I felt sitting next to you, the fact that I wanted to touch you, wanted you to touch me, and I found myself arguing with you just because it was more exciting and more fun than any interaction I'd ever had with any other man and it was all I could let myself have when I thought I'd made a prior commitment to somebody else."

His lips quirked in an unwilling smile. "You liked arguing with me?"

"Yes." Cass leaned closer and let her lips brush against his. "Good banter is like foreplay."

She drew back before she got carried away and forced herself to finish. "I didn't want Riley Adams to win after all he'd done to ruin my life. I didn't want to spend the rest of my life alone, either, and I was so tired of dating and not getting it right. I thought if I could find the right man online, we'd have a chance to get to know each other without being led astray by some shallow physical attraction, without Riley interfering, without me making the same mistakes I'd made in the past."

Cass looked at him with her heart in her eyes. "And it worked. I got you. Maybe the way it all worked out was a little confused and convoluted, but I'm not confused about how I feel."

"I'm not sure how I feel," Jason said. "I think you just called our relationship shallow."

She shook her head and felt the length of her hair sliding over her bare breasts with the movement. "There is nothing shallow about this attraction. I want you more than I've ever wanted anything in my life and I'll never stop wanting you."

He gave her a measuring look. "Even if I put the handcuffs on you and bring out the flogger?"

She couldn't help laughing. "Because that would be such a turn-off?"

Cass reached up and undid the catch, opening the

handcuffs, letting him loose to do his worst, or his best, whichever.

The last coherent thought she had was that no matter what else the future might hold for them, the sex was never going to be dull. Then Jason's hands were on her and there was no room for anything but feeling.

He cupped her breasts and she arched her back, pressing into his hold, offering more of herself. She felt her skin dance with electric awareness at his touch, felt the rush of need and want build under her skin. She moaned out loud when his fingers tugged at her nipples and her sex reacted as if he'd touched her there.

"Jason." She fell forward, falling into him, aware that she'd fallen for him well past the point of no return and she couldn't even say for sure when it had happened.

"Cass." He rolled with her, bringing her under him, the weight and heat of his body on hers heightening the ache inside her.

She arched under him, rocked her hips under his in an impatient demand, then sighed when she felt the press of his cock against her slick, ready flesh. "Hurry," she whispered.

His mouth found and claimed hers, his lips hungry and hot and possessive. She opened for him, letting his tongue sweep inside to taste her, deepening the kiss as he thrust slowly home.

She wound her legs around him and arched up to take more of him, too urgent to let him set a slower pace, needing him fast and hard and deep inside her. He took her mouth and her body with devastating thoroughness, leaving them both breathless, spent and sated an eternity of minutes later.

"I love you," Cass said when she was capable of speech again.

"Good." Jason levered himself up to look at her. "Don't walk out on me again."

"You're supposed to say you love me, too." She had a sudden awful thought. "Unless you don't."

"I do." His face was serious, his eyes dark with feeling and Cass felt her heart clutch in her chest.

"Oh. Good," she managed.

"In spite of the fact that you married me for money." A wicked light danced in his eyes. "You're going to have to make that up to me. Your turn to wear the handcuffs."

"We really have to send Mona a thank-you note for the wedding present," Cass said, feeling giddy and light and home at last.

She'd thought she'd lost everything, and now she had it all. Love, the beginnings of a new family, a home, the career of her dreams taking flight. The money almost seemed superfluous. Almost, but then again, Jason had mentioned renovating and expanding The Last Resort and she was going to shoot a lot of film with her new Holga.

"I think she's probably getting all the thanks she deserves right now," Jason said.

And then neither of them talked much for a long, long time.

About the Author

Charlene Teglia made her first novel sale in 2004. Since then her books have garnered several honors, including 2005 Romantic Times Reviewer's Choice Award for Best Erotic Novel, 2005 CAPA nomination for Best Erotic Anthology, and 2006 Romantic Times Top Reviewer's Choice nominee for Best Erotic Romance. When she's not writing, she can be found hiking around the Olympic Peninsula with her family or opening and closing doors for cats.

To learn more about Charlene Teglia, please visit www.charleneteglia.com.

They told themselves it was only for a month...

A Month From Miami
© *2008 Barbara Meyers*

Perrish, Florida was supposed to be just an eye-blink for Kaylee Walsh on her way to a glamorous new life in Miami-minus her sleazy ex-boyfriend. She's not about to let a little car trouble or an empty wallet throw a monkey wrench into her plans. Not even when there's a handsome mechanic on the other end of that wrench.

Rick Braddock knows better than to give a second glance to a woman with big-city dreams. But getting Kaylee back on the road means car repairs she can't afford. So he offers a trade. His services for hers. As a babysitter and housekeeper, that is.

They tell themselves it's only for a month. But as they settle into comfortably domestic days and intensely intimate nights, Rick realizes what a treasure he's discovered in Kaylee. And for Kaylee, the lure of Miami is losing its shine.

Then Rick discovers a fortune in stolen gems hidden in her gas tank. Is Kaylee the woman he thought she was-or is she taking him for a ride?

Warning: This title contains blowing and swallowing (of bubble gum), engines overheating with sexual tension, and explicit love scenes featuring superior handling and mind-blowing torque.

Available now in ebook and print from Samhain Publishing.

A lesson in seduction that releases lightning in a bottle…

All Bottled Up
© *2009 Christine d'Abo*

Call center worker Viola White makes a living selling dream vacations. Too bad her own life is a litany of unfilled fantasies. Prime example—the boss she pines for barely knows she exists. Now that she's won a trip to a Mexican beach resort, though, she vows to shake things up. Instead she winds up alone, empty handed and with a sore toe from the beautiful bottle she's tripped over.

A bottle that's purple, gold—and stuffed with over six feet of blue-eyed, black-haired hunk. If anyone could teach her how to seduce her boss, it's this sexy genie.

Jerod can't believe his bad luck. Three thousand years of granting frivolous wishes, and now he's stuck playing matchmaker. A series of sensual lessons later, he finds there's something different about this shy Viola. Something that tempts him to try to break free of his curse and make a life for himself—with her.

All he has to do is convince Viola that the man of her dreams is a dud. And the right man for the job of loving her is a genie.

Warning: May cause spontaneous wish fulfillment, eye rolls, and a bad case of the giggles. No bottles were harmed in the writing of this novel.

Available now in ebook from Samhain Publishing.